"Look at me, Karen."

Karen raised her eyes to David's. Her grip on the arms of her chair tightened—not at what she saw, but at the terrible tension in him. Rejection was what he clearly expected to get from her, as he had from others.

Feeling as if she were invading his territory, she inched forward into the pool of light. "Does it hurt?"

"Does it—" He couldn't hide his surprise. And finally replied with a wry smile, "No one has ever thought to ask."

That tension, and now the hint of vulnerability, drew Karen like a magnet. She moved close enough to touch him. But only when she looked at David's downbent head did she yield to the impulse to gently stroke his slightly scarred cheek. "Your scars—they look so much worse to you than they do to me," she murmured.

David only shook his head, the action bringing his lips into her palm for a kiss that made her tingle. . . .

Binnie Syril's second Temptation was actually the first romance she ever wrote, and we're glad that *Out of the Darkness* is now seeing the light of day. It was runner-up in the Romance Writers of America Golden Heart Contest in 1988. A voracious reader herself and a former librarian, Binnie has developed a true love for the written word, now being expressed through her own dramatic and moving stories. Binnie shares living quarters with her Brittany spaniel, Max, in Baltimore.

Books by Binnie Syril Braunstein

HARLEQUIN TEMPTATION
247–COLOUR OF LOVE

Out of the Darkness

BINNIE SYRIL

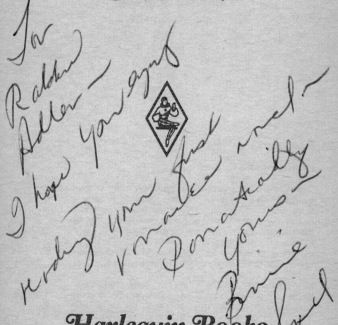

For
Robbin
Adler—
I hope your agent
reading your first
make model
Romatically
yours
Binnie
Syril
11/95

Harlequin Books

TORONTO • NEW YORK • LONDON
AMSTERDAM • PARIS • SYDNEY • HAMBURG
STOCKHOLM • ATHENS • TOKYO • MILAN

To my agent,
Linda Hayes,
for believing in
Karen and David
as I did.

And to my editor,
Lisa Boyes,
who also believed—
and pushed so hard
to bring this book
to the light of day.

Published November 1989

ISBN 0-373-25376-1

1

SOUNDS WOKE HIM—sounds that didn't belong. Sounds of soft, rustling footsteps through piles of autumn leaves. No one belonged here in the dark of his own private world. His private hell. The footsteps died at the edge of the garden, near the last of the roses. He was so groggy that he could barely force his eyes open. In the darkness a shadowy figure paused, bending to smell the flowers.

Angrily he inserted muscular forearms into the cuffs of the aluminum crutches that lent his body a functional but less-than-graceful mobility. He stood, balancing carefully, and flicked on an outdoor spotlight that threw the outlines of the garden into sharp relief. And for the first time he was able to see the short, slightly built intruder, who wore an oversize cap. The cap went flying as the figure backed away slightly, one arm raised as if to ward off the brightness of the light.

From behind the shelter of her raised forearm, Karen Anderson blinked at the spotlight that virtually blinded her while preventing her gaze from penetrating the darkened recesses of the patio.

"Who are you, and what the hell are you doing here?" David demanded as he advanced with measured steps toward the figure, realizing from the mass of blond hair and the glint of gold earrings that his intruder was a woman.

Karen, in turn, gave ground, unaccustomed frissons of alarm raising the hairs on the back of her neck as she heard the distinct note of menace in the man's deep voice, then heard him moving toward her. It never occurred to her that it took an inordinately long time for this very angry man to reach her. Instead, her mind tried to find reason despite her predicament.

Certainly this couldn't be the home of David Carter, her soon-to-be-colleague, she told herself as she looked down the path that separated what she could now see were two strands of rosebushes. Maybe she'd gotten the address wrong. Maybe the man moving inexorably toward her was a recluse, not the former foreign correspondent that Glen Larson, the managing editor of the Baltimore *Metropolitan*, had ordered her to meet—and work with.

She tried to recall what Larson had said in their brief and unprecedented meeting only that afternoon. Karen usually got her assignments through Alan Todd, the photo dispatcher. But when Larson had called to see her, she'd wasted no time in finding out what the man wanted. In newspapers, the managing editor was one short step away from God!

David Carter had been injured in the Middle East, Karen had learned from Larson, and he'd been out of action for more than a year, recuperating from a series of operations. Now the managing editor wanted the reporter back. So she, Karen, was being detached from her usual duties as a general assignment photographer to work with the man on a major, statewide series of articles. Her reward would be equal billing on the byline, a rare chance for advancement.

Karen had spent part of the day in the newspaper's library looking through clippings of David Carter's articles. Whether reporting local spot news or sending back dispatches of stories breaking in the Middle East, the man had a distinctively crisp, incisive writing style. She had looked forward to working with him. But now, as she surveyed the vaguely menacing figure standing in the shadows just outside the circle of light, she cursed her own stupidity in not calling ahead and verifying David Carter's address.

"I wouldn't go any farther down that garden path if I were you," the arrogant male voice advised her. "There's nothing behind you but brambles and woods. Ticks, too. And a rather steep drop."

The words "steep drop" sent shivers up and down her spine. She stopped dead. Waiting.

He could almost sense the fear emanating from her, and knew with a too-familiar, sick feeling that his presence was the cause of that fear. "Look, I'm sorry I shouted at you," he said resignedly. "Just—leave. Go back the way you came. I'll stay back here. You don't have to be afraid."

Something in that last word, or perhaps in the way the man had said it, caused Karen's fear to evaporate as if it had never been. "Why should I be afraid of you?" she asked.

He snorted in disbelief. "Tell me another one! You're afraid of what I look like!"

What an extraordinary thing to have said, Karen thought. "Look," she began patiently, as if to a child, "it's practically dark, and you're standing back in the shadows. I can't even see whether you're tall or short, light or dark. And even if I could, why should I care what you look like?"

And why should I bother to go into explanations? Why don't you just leave, lady, he pleaded silently as the night sounds colored the lengthening silence. Then, "Who are you and what are you doing here?" he asked wearily. He had his suspicions but he hoped they weren't true. Maybe the woman was simply a lost traveler or someone soliciting a contribution for the local volunteer fire department. She could even be one of his neighbors; he hadn't met any of them, after all.

"I'm Karen Anderson from the Baltimore *Metropolitan*. Are you David Carter?" She was hoping against hope that this unfriendly sounding man's answer would be "no."

"Yes, I'm David Carter. What do you want?"

To go home, have dinner and remind myself that tomorrow is another day! "I'm a photographer," she informed him in even tones. "Glen Larson sent me to talk to you about working on a long-term assignment. He said that he'd call you. I guess he didn't get around to it," she added, smothering a sigh.

"Yeah, he called."

"Then why aren't we talking about the job instead of standing here on a dark patio?" she demanded, one hand pushing at the loose knot of hair that persisted in trying to fall down around her shoulders.

"Larson's a dreamer, Ms Anderson. I told him that I wasn't interested—"

"Not interested!" She gasped in shock.

"You got it. Period. I also told him that sending anyone out here was a waste of time. And I'm not about to change my mind. So if you'd just leave . . ." he urged once more.

Karen groaned inwardly. She could see her vision of a byline going right down the tubes, along with her career at the *Met*, when Larson's editorial wrath descended. Her future would be a journalistic wasteland.

She struggled to control her rising temper; voicing her thoughts to her inhospitable colleague probably wouldn't gain her much.

"Is it because of me, personally, that you won't do the assignment? Is there a particular photographer you prefer working with? Or are you just too chauvinistic to want to work with a woman?" she demanded with a toss of her head.

He eyed the woman before him, who with her dark slacks, shapeless khaki jacket and blond hair escaping from the knot on her head, looked more like a street urchin than a professional journalist. "None of the above. I have nothing against you personally. Hell, I told Larson when he called that I was sticking to the book-and-author column I write, and that I wasn't about to get involved with anything else. And definitely not *with* anyone else. I work solo. It isn't as if he didn't know how I felt about the subject when he sent you out here. And now you know, too. So do us all a favor. Go home!"

She stood her ground, legs braced, fisted hands planted on her slender hips. "Look, I don't pretend to understand any of this, nor how I ended up in the middle of some feud between you and Larson, but I don't much like it, and I'm not amused! I've been up since six o'clock this morning. This is the first time all day that a camera's been out of my hands. My plans for this evening have been knocked into next week, not to mention the dinner that I haven't had. Common courtesy—"

"If you believed in common courtesy, you wouldn't be in my backyard without an invitation."

"I rang the doorbell."

"I didn't hear it."

"And why do I get the impression that even if you had, you wouldn't have moved from this spot to answer it?" she asked the man who loomed in the shadows.

"You have good instincts, lady. Are you that good with a camera in your hands?"

"My editor likes my work," she replied with a self-deprecating shrug.

"And Don Ross isn't easy, any more than Larson is."

"Don knows I don't give up on an assignment." No matter how unpleasant it might be, she added silently. Then, "Don't you think you owe me at least an explanation, if nothing else?"

"An explanation," he echoed, smothering a sigh. He didn't want more conversation; he wanted her to leave. But getting rid of Karen Anderson was proving far more difficult than he'd imagined it would be. By now he was resigned to the fact that he would have to tell her things he had no desire to share with anyone. At the same time he felt a certain grudging admiration, recognizing in her something that he himself had once had in spades—bulldog tenacity.

He wasn't about to step out of the darkness and forcibly send her on her way. He wouldn't do that to her; he hadn't sunk that low. But he had the uneasy feeling that if he didn't tell her what was really behind his refusing the assignment, she might very well camp on his patio all night.

"Sit down," he said finally. "Not there!" he barked as she walked toward a chair at the edge of the patio. "There's a stone bench just to your right, on the grass."

The hard edge in the man's voice stopped her in her tracks. Bending wearily to pick up her cap, she sank down onto the damp stone surface he'd indicated.

"All right. There is an assignment. Glen Larson, our beloved, Machiavellian managing editor, cooked it up for my benefit. And I'm not having any!"

"Why not?" she asked, amazed that anyone, even a former foreign correspondent, would have the nerve to defy the iron-willed Larson. "Don't you have to take the assignments you're given, just like the rest of us? And where do you get off saying you're 'not interested'?" she demanded, recalling what she'd heard him say earlier.

All the while he'd been talking to her, David had assumed that Karen, like other *Met* staffers, would have heard about what had happened to him. Could it be that his fame hadn't preceded him, that she really didn't know.... "Didn't Larson tell you about me—that I have a reason for living out here on the sidelines?"

"I've only been working with the paper for two years. All I know about you is that you have a column in the paper every other week. Mr. Larson told me you'd been in an accident in the Middle East, and in the hospital afterward...."

"That's an understatement," David muttered as he took a deep breath and retraced his steps to the unyielding wrought-iron bench. He sat down heavily, leaning his head against the cool roughness of the brick wall behind him. "I was in the Middle East for more than a year as a correspondent for the paper. I'd worked my way up from spot news to covering a beat, but what I really wanted was to be assigned overseas. I worked my tail off. I didn't care whether I was sent to a war zone or not; I couldn't wait to get on that plane."

He closed his eyes briefly, as if that would prevent searing memories from flashing through his mind in living color. He swallowed hard. "Well, one day I was in a Jeep, in a supposedly neutral area. Only a rocket launcher didn't know that. The Jeep ended up as so much junk." He didn't tell her what had happened to the people with him—the driver, the United Press International photographer, the correspondent from one of the cable networks. "I didn't come off much better than the Jeep."

Karen clutched the edge of the hard stone bench, shivering not at its penetrating dampness, but at the bitterness that textured David's voice.

"I—I thought it would be just a matter of time before I'd be able to go back to where and what I was before I left Maryland," David said in a low voice.

"Why can't you?" Karen asked gently, virtually hypnotized by his softly spoken narrative.

David retrieved the forearm crutches, putting them on with a motion made fluid through long practice. As he stood up, his body protested silently against the stiffness caused by sitting too long in the damp Maryland night. "A street reporter has to be able to hare off after spot news. Instantly. These—" he swallowed hard, gesturing toward his legs and the crutches, though she couldn't see them "—these crutches are not conducive to spot news. And my legs are held together with baling wire."

She heard creaks as he stood tantalizingly outside the periphery of her vision, his weight shifting back and forth as he balanced himself. Why was the man giving her insights that breached the very barriers he'd worked so long and hard to erect? And why was he so embarrassed to be seen using a pair of crutches?

She listened to his deep, sometimes rough baritone, all the while trying to judge from its sound the height of the body that went with the voice. She itched to move forward, to see for herself what he was so obviously afraid that she would see. But something held her back. There was an invisible boundary that David Carter himself had created, and which Karen, in all good conscience and compassion, could not cross. She fought to keep her lively journalistic curiosity on a tight leash. "Couldn't you work from a desk? Do editorial work?" she pressed, forgetting for the moment that her purpose was to convince him to work with her.

"I can't. I have no right to impose on other people."

She almost had to strain to hear his words. "Impose." That didn't make any sense. Larson must have wanted David Carter back pretty badly. Why else would he have gone to the effort of sending her out to see him? But when she said as much to David, she could almost hear his shrug as he replied that Larson was a good guy, and an old friend.

Here David paused, shifting slightly. "As my boss, he has a copy of my medical reports. But he hasn't seen me since I came back."

"Why not?" Karen asked, remembering that Larson had told her David Carter had undergone a series of operations. She wondered if Larson was one of those people who couldn't tolerate illness in others.

"I haven't wanted to see anyone. Glen's respected that, up until now. And if he *had* seen me, I doubt if he'd want me back downtown," David concluded with a heavy sigh.

"I don't understand. You say you don't walk very easily, but that's certainly not difficult for anyone to accept. And the building's barrier-free."

David cursed bitterly, the sound harsh even to his own ears as he mentally damned the woman whose presence had forced him to say as much as he had already. "The Jeep was turned into flying pieces of shrapnel. And—" Here he paused, because the rest wasn't easy to put into words. "It wasn't only my legs that were injured." He swallowed convulsively. "At least that part of me was protected by fatigues. My face wasn't so lucky."

"Your face!" Karen gasped, barely aware that she'd spoken.

"Yeah. Anyway, since I got back more than a year ago, this house and a few hospital rooms have been my whole world."

"You don't see *anyone?*" she asked incredulously. *What about family,* she wanted to ask. *Friends? A lover? What happens when the aloneness gets to be too much? Or are you so immune to the human frailties that plague the rest of us?* The questions were all there, screaming to be asked. But she said nothing.

"No, I don't see anyone," he said finally. "Not since I was released from in-hospital therapy. And no one sees me. That's the way I want it. And that's the way it's going to stay. I don't need anyone. I can make it on my own."

She was appalled. "But surely—"

"Ms Anderson, you haven't walked in my shoes. You can't know what it's like to come up to someone— someone you care about—and see that person cringe. I hope you never know that feeling. I've been burned, lady, literally and figuratively speaking. Hell, can you imagine my walking up to an unsuspecting interview subject? I'm not up to seeing eyes lower in embarrassment or, worse yet, watching people turn away in shock. Thanks a lot, but no thanks! Not anymore!"

"What if Larson won't take no for an answer?" she asked, shaken by the bitterness of the man's words.

"I'll quit," she heard him say, and from the lack of hesitation in his voice, she knew he meant it. The words so quietly and decisively spoken chilled her.

"Don't you care about the paper anymore? You fought so hard to get where you were."

"The paper gets along just fine the way it is. And so do I."

"It's such a waste," she said, shaking her head, knowing all too well what the waste of a life—or lives— could mean.

"It's my life," he retorted. "Tell me, do you usually try to reform people you haven't even seen?"

She could feel her face grow warm and was relieved that he was too far back in the shadows to notice. "Sure, I have a do-gooder complex. Oh, come on. I'm not trying to reform you. I'm just trying to work with you!"

"Why?" he demanded bluntly.

"Will you change your mind if I tell you?" she asked hopefully.

In spite of the fact that he knew the answer, David's curiosity was aroused. "Try it and see. I'm always willing to listen," came the noncommittal reply.

"I'd be someone to bounce ideas off," she began.

"I'm used to working on my own."

"Working with someone else might give your writing a new perspective."

"There's something wrong with my writing?"

"No, but aren't you ever tired of doing book pieces?"

"No."

"You don't think you could be getting a little—stale?"

"Not that I'd noticed," he said drily.

"I could dig for information, like you used to."

"I do my own digging by long distance. Is that it?" he asked, fascinated despite himself at the enthusiasm he heard in her voice and at the persistence of the rapid-fire verbal artillery she was hurling at him.

No, that's not it, she answered silently. She had one more shot but didn't know if she had the courage to take it. It would mean appealing to David Carter's better nature—and from what she'd heard so far, she wasn't sure he had one. She would have to dredge up the courage to lay herself bare, make herself vulnerable to this man she didn't know. She would just have to take the chance.

She took a deep breath. "My work is the most important thing in my life." Without her job at the *Met*, she might not have gotten through the past two years. She didn't work to live, she acknowledged bleakly. She lived to work. "Working with you, with a reporter of your calibre, on a project like this one, might open up the way for me to get other top assignments," she told him frankly.

"Ah, the lady's a careerist."

"It takes one to know one," she retorted.

"Touché. You're honest, anyway." He laughed without humor. "And I'm sorry that I can't give that career of yours a boost, Karen."

"Wait a minute!" She cut into his obvious farewell speech. "You said if I told you why I wanted to work with you, you might change your mind. I kept my part of the bargain. Why don't you keep yours?" she challenged, firing what she knew would probably be the last shot in her verbal arsenal.

"I only said I'd be willing to listen. I never said I would change my mind."

"Thanks for being so open-minded," she ground out.

"Look, I know you must be disappointed." Hell, her fiery enthusiasm so intrigued him that against his will, *he* was disappointed, too. The best thing—for both of them—would be to get it over with. "I'm sorry—I really am. And I'm sorry about your wasted trip, and the dinner you haven't eaten, and the date that got messed up."

"Date?" she put in, wondering where he'd gotten that idea.

"You said you had plans for this evening. I just assumed you had a date."

"No date," she snapped. "Hotshot investigative reporters shouldn't make reckless assumptions, Mr. Carter." She wasn't about to tell him that her "date" was with the pool at the Y. Swimming tired her to the point that on some nights, at least, she was able to sleep without getting caught in the quicksand of nightmare. In a way, her existence was almost as solitary as his own, at least in the ways that mattered.

From the curtness of her response and the flatness of her tone, he could tell that the reference to her social life had hurt her in some way. Maybe she didn't go out at all. He shouldn't have brought the subject up. Certainly it was none of his business how she spent her after-work hours, and he knew all too well how rejection felt. "I'm sorry. I didn't mean to ridicule your plans for tonight. And as for your trip out here, you'll have to take it up with Larson. Maybe he can authorize some time off for you to make up for your wasted evening."

"Right. I'm really looking forward to telling Larson about our meeting tonight. I just can't wait!" And no matter what she finally told Larson, she knew damned well she wouldn't be asking the man for any time off; that was the last thing she wanted! "Well," she sighed, "I guess this is partially my fault for not checking with you before I came out here. But since the boss said he'd take care of everything, I never thought to question him. Nobody questions him. So much for blind obedience!" she concluded wryly as she got up from the bench. "Good night, Mr. Carter," she said softly, and retraced her steps to her car.

"Goodbye, Ms Anderson." His response was automatic as he heard the echoes of his visitor's footsteps grow fainter, then heard the grating sound of an engine starting up. He edged his hand up the brick wall behind him, finding the switch and flicking off the patio light. The darkness returned. So did the quiet. But the quality of the silence wasn't quite the same, not after the presence of his intruder. Neither was the all-enveloping, dark solitude that had been a numbing drug to his senses for so long.

DAVID CARTER wore his aloneness like a cloak, Karen told herself as she drove the silent roads back to Baltimore. He was steeped in it—hadn't willingly been face-to-face with another human being in more than a year. Karen shivered, her hands tightening reflexively on the steering wheel. He'd virtually condemned himself to living out his life in solitary confinement. Only there were no visible guards and no restraints, except for the ones he imposed on himself.

The thought of David Carter was an invisible companion that haunted Karen as, minutes later, she let herself into her two-bedroom apartment on Federal Hill. She was alone, too, but not in the same way as the man who was determined to live his life in the shadows. She was lonely; he was not. Why should that bother her, she wondered, more than a little annoyed with herself. After all, it was clearly none of her business. What had become of her carefully cultivated detachment?

Once she was inside her apartment, Karen made a beeline for the kitchen. Maybe a good meal would divert her thoughts from the evening's failure and the man responsible for it. As she munched on cold roast chicken and a tossed green salad, she tried to focus on something constructive: the explanation she was going to give Glen Larson the next morning. She was barely able to control a shudder at the thought of it.

But dinner, and even the slice of chocolate cake that she had for dessert, did nothing to help her with a solution to her problem. The best thing would be to put the whole situation on a mental back burner, she decided as she cleared away the remnants of her meal.

Turning her back on the kitchen, Karen determinedly put aside all thoughts of Larson, Carter and shadowy men in dark places. Instead she indulged her love of music by putting up her feet and immersing herself in half an hour of Bach. Tim had loved the mathematical precision and purity of the great baroque composer, Karen recalled, her gaze automatically seeking and finding the framed photograph on the coffee table.

Most people would have had a wedding portrait on display. But Karen had liked their second anniversary picture even better. She'd taken the picture of Tim on the beach in Ocean City. The camera had caught his fun-loving spirit as he'd struggled to launch a kite.

She glanced again at the picture. Time would never be able to add anything to the perfection of the photograph, or to the gloss of memory. There would never be lines of strain, hurt, worry, sorrow, grief there.

Those lines were etched on her own portrait, the one she saw every time she looked in her mirror.

Karen shut off the stereo, leaving Bach for another night. But while the luxury of a long soak in the tub helped to relieve her physical tiredness, it did little to ease the familiar ache of loss, pain and the absence of love. Even after nearly two years, it hurt, she acknowledged readily, the fingers of her right hand automatically seeking the still-bright gold band that graced the ring finger of her left hand. All their love had ended in the Catoctin Mountains, not long after that photograph had been taken. She had never been back there since.

Karen shivered, realizing that the bath water had long since grown cold. She climbed out of the tub, reaching for a fluffy, rose-colored bath sheet. She used a corner of it to wipe away tears, then wrapped the length of terry around her body, a smaller towel around her hair. She dried herself quickly, watching her image grow clearer as the steam on the bathroom mirror dissipated.

The mirror, like the camera's lens, didn't lie, Karen acknowledged dispassionately as she removed the larger of the two towels. At twenty-eight, she had a figure much the same as Tim had always liked it, trim and neat. Her high, firm breasts had always seemed to fill his hands. Loving hands. And the softness of her slender figure had always seemed to fit naturally into the hard, muscular ranginess of his body. Even now, she ached for him. Only him. Because in the time since his death, she had never been able to find anyone to replace him. She hadn't even looked.

Karen reached behind the bathroom door, removing a knee-length, satin sleep shirt from its hook. She slipped it over her head, then towel-dried her hair before drying it with a blow-dryer. Her hair came halfway down to her waist if she didn't pin it up. It was almost always piled into a knot on top of her head, then bundled into a cap, keeping it out of the way when she was working.

She flicked off the bathroom light, then padded silently into her darkened bedroom. Despite everything she was lucky, she told herself as she slid between cool, crisp sheets. Although nothing could make up for losing Tim and for the awful emptiness that had followed, she at least had her parents. They'd offered her a home, but they understood her need to make it on her own in her chosen profession. Still, they were always there, ready to offer what support they could, any way that they could.

What about David Carter? she wondered as she closed her eyes. Did he have someone who cared enough about him to break through the barriers he'd erected?

Karen tried to imagine what it would be like, living alone, not seeing anyone. She remembered her own hard-fought battles with grief and loneliness, of times when the darkness of her apartment made her feel almost claustrophobic. Those times weren't in the forgotten past; they still happened. She was glad that her parents were only a phone call away, just south of Annapolis, and that she would see the faces of friends, or even strangers, when she went to work the next day.

When Tim had been alive, her career had meshed with her marriage. But in the time since his death she'd focused much of her energy—daytime, nighttime and weekends, too, when necessary—on her job at the *Metropolitan*. For some reason she couldn't quite understand, she was deeply sorry that David Carter had locked himself away. Her mind was churning on some deeper level, trying to find a key to the door.

HER NIGHT WAS A STRING of restless hours; there had been no swim at the YWCA pool to dull the edges of tiredness. Her dreams were not of Tim, as they had so often been in the past, but of a man who looked as if he were locked in a cage. He never seemed to turn so that she could see his face. The image persisted, not even disappearing when she awoke before the ring of her alarm clock.

"Come on, Karen," she muttered, annoyed at her dreamlike Man in the Iron Mask, as she labeled him. "You're getting obsessed with a man who won't even agree to see you, much less work with you! You aren't interested in men that you can see; why should you be interested in one that you can't? Put him out of your mind!"

2

MANILA FOLDERS tucked under her arm, Karen stopped first the next morning at the glass-enclosed office of *Met* librarian Michelle "Mickie" Lewin. Mickie was one of the first people Karen had met after joining the paper. She'd done Karen a big favor by pulling the mass of David Carter clippings the day before, and then allowed her to borrow them overnight. Karen had no reason to keep them any longer; somebody else might be needing them. And besides, she told herself wryly, it would postpone the inevitable confrontation with Larson for that much longer.

Mickie got up from her desk as soon as she saw Karen coming toward her.

"Thanks for pulling these for me," Karen said as she handed the folders back to the other woman.

"No problem. Did you find what you were looking for?"

For a moment Karen hardly knew how to answer the question. She did know that she had an inordinate degree of curiosity about someone she would never work with—would never even see. But now that she knew as much as she did, it was hard to close the door on the man. She really *did* want to work with him. "They were a starting point," she said halfheartedly.

"You doing a photo essay on the guy?"

The ultimate irony of the question cut deeply. Imagine David Carter allowing anyone to take a picture of him! "No, nothing like that," she said with a sigh. Then, "Mickie, what's he like?"

"You mean what *was* he like?" Mickie asked, glancing at Karen sharply.

"Yes. I guess that is what I mean."

"All this—the files—the question—it isn't idle curiosity, is it?"

"You know I wouldn't take up your time for nothing."

"Have you got time for a cup of coffee?"

When Karen said yes, she found herself in a chair, a mug of steaming black coffee in front of her and a plate of cookies within easy reach.

"Okay, lady. Give," Mickie demanded. "Are you switching from photo to reporting and doing a piece on Dave as a spring board?"

"Hardly!" Karen laughed. "I can't write. I take pictures with a camera, I don't describe them in words. Besides, it's against company policy to do stories on our own people unless they've done something extraordinary, like win a Pulitzer Prize—"

"Or get creamed in some Middle Eastern hellhole," Mickie muttered into her coffee cup.

"That, too," Karen agreed softly. "Mr. Larson mentioned something about my working with David Carter. . . ."

At that, Mickie leaned back in her swivel chair, one eyebrow raised in an unspoken question. "I didn't think he'd come back to work yet."

And if it were up to him, he never would! "He hasn't," Karen sighed. "That's why it's ninety-eight percent certain that the assignment won't fly." She didn't bother to tell Mickie that David had turned it down flat. "Tell me about the man. I might never get to work with him, and I certainly can't ask Larson anything."

"Why do you want to know?"

"I hardly know myself," she replied. It had been aeons since anything—anyone—had affected her so deeply. Any *man*, she forced herself to admit grudgingly. "All I can say is, ever since I went out to his place last night I haven't been able to get him out of my mind."

Mickie sat forward in her chair. "You went out to his place in the Valley?"

She nodded. "Yes, on Larson's orders."

"And did you see Dave?"

"No. He didn't want to see me or even to let me get too close to him."

"I'm not surprised," Mickie said. "I've talked to him quite a bit over the telephone since he got back. He always needs research material for his columns. He seems pretty well set on staying out there in the country."

He is that, Karen agreed silently, not wanting to interrupt Mickie's train of thought.

"Okay. David Carter. He is—or was—a careerist, totally dedicated to the profession. He would and did go just about anywhere—and to any lengths—for a story. He was really intense, almost as if he were out to prove something. But at the same time he didn't walk all over people. For example, he was always courteous to the library staff, returned clipping files on time and with nothing missing. He even allowed lead time when he needed materials that weren't in-house. He's—well, I guess the best way to summarize is to say that he's a decent guy, and that what happened after he went to the Middle East is a damned shame."

"After he went...you mean, the attack on his Jeep?"

"That, too, of course. But what I really meant was Eleanor Hanson. She worked for the paper. She and Dave were definitely an item. But when he came back in pieces . . ."

"She dumped him? Because of—his face?" Karen asked reluctantly.

"Not exactly," Mickie said, a mirthless twist of a smile on her lips. "Eleanor was a jet-setter, a real high-flier. She was into skiing in the winter, tennis in the summer. She didn't have time to wait around for a guy who was going to be flat on his back for a long time. She ditched him for someone who meshed with her life-style."

Karen winced. No wonder the man was so reluctant to expose himself to something or someone new. "Why do you suppose Larson sent me in cold, not telling me how bad David's condition really was? Aside from upsetting the person I was supposed to see, I made a fool of myself."

"*That* I seriously doubt. There are four photographers on the staff here. Dave's been at the paper long enough to have worked with three of them. By the time you came to work here two years ago, he was already posted overseas. Maybe Larson didn't want you to have any preconceived notions. Who can tell what goes on in the Great Man's mind? But Karen . . ." Here Mickie paused, a frown creasing her forehead. "If you do work with Dave, go easy."

"What does that mean?"

"You and Dave aren't so different. You're pretty intense yourself, and not overly anxious to let anybody get close to you."

"I get along fine with Don Ross—"

"Who's been married for ten years and happens to be your boss. You're also perfectly at ease with Scott, my beloved other half. But they're both 'safe.' What about the eligible guys—say, Jack Dailey?"

Karen's green eyes narrowed at the thought of the arrogant, Greek-god handsome reporter who thought widows were "easy." She had no intention of getting involved with Jack, or with any other man like him.

"If I were forced to sit this close to Jack Dailey on a regular basis," she told Mickie, "I'd have even more in common with your friend David Carter. I'd want to use the telephone, too! Anyway, the whole question of my working with David is pretty much a moot point. From our little talk last night, it was all too clear that he's not about to do the assignment, regardless of Larson's orders to the contrary. Thanks for the coffee and conversation, and for pulling all the stuff for me," she said as she set the mug on the corner of Mickie's desk.

"Dave's reaction isn't personal," the librarian said, unknowingly repeating what David himself had said the night before. "He's frustrated as hell and really down on himself, and that makes him doubly wary of outside contacts. Are you open to a farfetched idea?" she asked just as Karen reached the door to the library office.

"Shoot," Karen said, turning to face the other woman.

"Do you really want to work with him?"

"Yes!"

Mickie smothered a grin at Karen's lack of hesitation.

"He does all of his interviews by phone. What's to prevent him from working on this assignment with you the same way?"

For a long moment Karen just stared. Then, "Mickie, did I ever tell you that you're a genius?"

"Hey, he hasn't said yes yet."

"He will," Karen muttered darkly. "Do you mind if I use your phone?"

"Sure, go ahead," Mickie replied with a nod, obligingly leaving her office so that Karen could have some privacy.

She reached for the staff telephone directory on Mickie's desk. But she stopped just short of picking up the receiver. What right did she have to intrude on the man's life? Oh, sure, working with him would be a terrific opportunity for her, but she'd surely manage to work her way up the ladder without him.

DAVID CARTER FLEXED tired shoulder muscles, then leaned back in his chair. He'd spent most of a sleepless night thinking about the uninvited guest who had turned up on his patio. Damn Glen Larson, anyway. If he hadn't come up with that cockamamy idea of his, Karen Anderson never would have shown up here. And what a masterful story Larson had created, David thought, shaking his head in grudging admiration as he recalled their conversation.

"I want you to pick up the slack, Dave," Larson had said, the puffing of his ever-present pipe audible even over the phone. "Maryland beat reporter Ellen Johnson has received a Curtin Fellowship, and she'll be spending the next six months at the Columbia School of Journalism. You can start with a new state-of-the-state series. You know—who and what are the most important people and places, and how and why did they get that way."

"That sounds like a magazine feature piece, not a news item."

"I don't care what it sounds like, as long as it gets written. By you. You'll be working with a photographer—"

His unhesitating answer had been, "No, thanks."

"You intend to work solo?" Larson had wanted to know.

"I intend to continue what I've been doing—writing book-and-author columns from my desk out here."

Larson's end of the line had been silent for a time, after which the managing editor had spoken with deceptive softness. "Dave, I think you've known me long enough to know that I don't usually make explanations. I've given you one: we're down one reporter and we need you to fill in. I don't recall offering you an option." With that, Larson had hung up.

The insistent ringing of the telephone derailed David's train of thought. "No loss," he muttered, shaking his head at the piece he was working on, which just didn't seem to hang together. He reached for the phone, fully expecting to hear Larson's roar. "Carter," he said.

"This is—Karen Anderson," came the rather hesitant voice from the other end of the line. When there was no answer, she took a deep breath and continued, "I came to your house last night, if you remember."

"I remember." *Only too well*, he added silently. He'd been up half the night trying to forget! Her voice alone, with all its nuances of annoyance, temper, even compassion, had echoed in his head. They had certainly struck sparks off each other; the verbal fireworks had lit up the night sky. She'd so intrigued him that if things had been . . . different it might have been interesting to see what the results would be. It was as if his self-imposed isolation had contracted an invasive virus named Karen Anderson. She'd been impossible to erase from his mind. "Did Larson give you a hard time when you told him it was no go?"

Stalling for time, she bit into a cookie with a crunch.

"What is that?" David demanded.

"What?"

"That sound, that grinding noise. Is there a giant termite somewhere on the line?"

She nearly choked on a combination of crumbs and a surprised gurgle of laughter. Somewhere underneath all that bitterness, David Carter had a sense of humor! "Cookie," she sputtered.

"Why do I get the impression you're always hungry? Even last night you were mumbling something about missing dinner."

"It's not that I'm always hungry. It's just that I'm always eating on the run, or sometimes not at all. And then when I finally do get to eat, I'm usually ravenous. Sometimes it's downright embarrassing. My mother says I have a tapeworm. She spent most of my childhood trying to get me to gain weight. It never worked," she babbled nervously.

So the body that had worn the shapeless jacket and loose-fitting slacks the night before was slender. "I'm impressed," he said with a laugh.

His laugh had a rich, if rusty sound, as if he didn't laugh very often. "Glad to hear it. Now about the assignment."

"Back to that again, are you?" he asked wryly.

"I've got an idea," she prodded gently, twisting the phone cord around nervous fingers. "And I really do want to work with you."

"I think you lost me somewhere. I thought we were in agreement that I was not working with you on Larson's pet project!"

Bolstered by Mickie Lewin's suggestion, Karen ignored David's last outburst and forged ahead. "You said last night that you don't see anyone and that you do the work for your columns by telephone, right?"

"What does that have to do with anything?"

"Just answer the question."

"Right," he agreed. "And my research materials are delivered by courier from the paper. The results vary, depending on who's doing the digging at that end."

"Then I don't see why we can't work together," she informed him brightly. "We can do it all by telephone."

At first David was simply dumbfounded. He stared at the telephone in his hand as if he'd never seen it before. "Are you singularly obtuse, or don't you know how to take no for an answer? If you're not hearing me in English, I can switch to French, Arabic or Hebrew."

"Did you go to Berlitz before you shipped out for the Middle East?" she quipped, more than happy that he couldn't see the deep flush of embarrassment that his words brought to her cheeks.

"I used Foreign Service tapes. Karen—"

"I guess I'm not good on taking no for an answer in any language. Look, David," she rushed on, "I could do all the background shots, and whatever else was necessary. I'd deliver the prints to you. We wouldn't have to see each other any more than you see your usual interview subjects, or the *Met*'s courier." She paused to allow him to digest what she'd said, holding her breath all the while.

"It wouldn't work."

She had to clamp her lips shut for a moment so as not to tell him in very graphic terms what she thought of his extremely negative attitude. "I'll even do your research for you. I know how to dig for facts, and I don't mind doing it. And I'm a good photographer," she added.

"It's not that. I'm not questioning your credentials. It's just that I value my privacy."

"I wouldn't make any attempt to infringe on that privacy, or try to catch you unawares. I have a lot of self-control. You could be standing right next to me, and I wouldn't look up to see you unless you specifically requested that I do so."

"Do you really mean that?"

"I really mean that," she confirmed. "And I don't lie."

"I don't think Larson will go for it."

Clutching at straws, aren't you Mr. Reporter, Karen asked silently. Aloud she said, "Larson told me to work with you, not look at you. All he wants is copy. If we—" she found that she liked the sound of the word "—if we give him his articles, somehow I don't think he'll care whether you got your information face-to-face or via mental telepathy!"

"You'll have to do a lot of solo traveling," he warned.

So far he hadn't said no.... "I'm used to it. My travel time to your house in the Worthington Valley yesterday wasn't exactly short, you know."

"All right. I'll concede that your idea might work. I'll give it a try." If nothing else, it would keep Larson off his back for a while.

"Terrific! Starting when?"

"I'll sit down tonight and put together what I need. In the meantime, you can give me a visual tour through

Baltimore and the surrounding counties. There's a lot that I haven't seen in a year and more."

"Right. I'll drop the prints by as soon as they're ready."

"No!" The last thing he needed was for Karen Anderson to be turning up on his doorstep every other day. "I mean, don't bother to make a special trip out here. Just send everything by courier."

He didn't want her back at his house, that much was all too obvious. Which clearly meant that he hadn't decided to trust her—yet. Well, she would win that trust, she vowed. "Then I'll hear from you after you've seen the prints?"

"Right. You're going to be one busy lady!"

"How did it go?" Mickie Lewin asked.

She had hung up the phone but hadn't yet moved from the chair, so great was her relief at David's agreeing to her plan. "He said he'll give it a try," she said, looking up at Mickie with a tremulous smile.

"Way to go, kid! By the way, I thought you might like to have a look at the cover story in this back copy of *Metro-Lights*.

On the front cover of the *Met*'s in-house newspaper, she saw a photograph of a ruggedly good-looking man in battle fatigues and combat boots. He was standing by a dusty, battered Jeep, his thick, dark hair tousled and windblown. There were laugh lines around his eyes and vertical grooves bracketing his smiling mouth. What color were his eyes? she wondered automatically. Despite the loose-fitting clothes, she got an overall impression of whipcord muscularity and controlled strength. The picture was a black-and-white still image, but the man in it seemed filled with energy, bubbling over with restless vitality. She could almost see him running after a story. Running. *Oh, God,* she groaned inwardly. The caption read: "Carter Gets Middle East Post."

"So this is David Carter," she breathed.

"No, Karen," Mickie corrected gently. "That *was* David Carter."

"Thanks, I think," she managed, wondering if she would ever find out how close David Carter's past image came to his present self.

"Keep it. I've got another one. But I wouldn't tell him that you saw it."

"Don't worry, I won't," Karen agreed as she slipped it into her gadget bag.

Later that night, she put the issue of *Metro-Lights* on her coffee table, not far from the picture of Tim. "The men in my life," she murmured, shaking her head sadly. She might not be able to see David Carter in person, but now, at least, she had some sense of his physical presence.

DURING THE NEXT THREE WEEKS Karen's itinerary included Baltimore and the surrounding counties, the Eastern Shore, Western Maryland and the area that bordered the Pennsylvania line. And it seemed that every time the phone rang, it was David, often apologetic but always with a directive that sent her and her Nikons to yet another part of the state. "I feel like I'm preparing a travel brochure," she finally told him. "At this rate, I'll be doing this until next spring."

And as if worrying about David's slow start weren't bad enough, too often she had Glen Larson to contend with. She couldn't very well duck him when he appeared in her doorway or cornered her in a hall. All she got for her efforts was his shark-tooth smile and the inevitable, "How's it coming?"

To which she would reply, "Still in the research stage," automatically covering for David as well as herself.

"I need retakes of some of the city shots," her unseen colleague told her curtly late one Friday afternoon.

"Why?" she asked resignedly as visions of a relaxing weekend catching up with her own free-lance work began disappearing into a haze.

"They're too pretty. Baltimore never looked that good in its young life. Let me have some grit. And shots six through eleven were taken in the afternoon. I want to see morning light."

She stared blankly at the phone in her hand. "Why?"

"It should be obvious. There were shadows."

Shadows. He wanted her to redo virtually all the shots she'd taken. No matter how hard she tried, she wasn't giving him what he wanted or needed in the way of photographic support. That shook her confidence and shattered her self-esteem. "The pictures aren't all for publication. They're to orient you and let you be on location without actually leaving your home," she informed him through gritted teeth, striving to keep a tight rein on her temper.

"Do you want to work with me or not?"

"Yes!" she hissed. "When do you want to see the retakes?"

"I'd like to have them by Monday afternoon. I'm sorry if that's going to mess up your weekend."

I'll just bet you are. "Don't worry about it." She wasn't about to tell him that her weekend plans consisted only of a visit to her parents' home. After three unrewarding weeks of working with this character, she certainly could have used the break!

"YOU HAVE A DATE?" Dorothy Sturgis asked her daughter hopefully when told of the change in plans for the coming weekend.

For a brief moment Karen considered letting her mother think she was going out. The untruth died unsaid. "I'm working with a reporter on an assignment."

"Well, don't work too hard. And remember, we do have a daughter, even if she hasn't been home in so long that it's hard to remember what she looks like. Keep in touch."

"Yes, Mom." Karen laughed wryly. Later, when she had some time, she would do a comic self-portrait photo and put it in the mail to the folks. Just to remind them what their daughter looked like. Maybe she would dress in something striped and make it up to look like a mug shot. She could make a copy for David Carter at the same time with the subtitle, Karen Anderson, Indentured to David Carter....

SATURDAY MORNING saw her leaving her apartment before dawn, her tripod set up on a sidewalk and her light meter telling her what she needed to know. People walked by, and she held her breath, silently urging them to hurry. Her eyes were gritty from too little sleep and too much aggravation. "Will Larson let me requisition toothpicks for my eyes?" she grumbled to herself as she changed lenses.

She spent all of Sunday in her darkroom, her sole objective a set of prints that would satisfy David. By the end of the day her head was filled with fumes from developer fluid, her eyes were semipermanently tinted red from the darkroom bulb and her temper oscillated between ferocious and apoplectic.

She gave the shots to the courier on Monday morning; they would be delivered in the afternoon. She heaved a sigh of relief. But on Tuesday, she received yet another call, this time asking her to go back down to Southern Maryland and then out to Frederick once more.

"That's it!" she exploded then and there at the *Met* offices, grabbing the prints David had returned, as well as all her photographic paraphernalia. She left the building at top speed. Perhaps if she talked to him in person, they could resolve what was obviously a serious communication problem. Once and for all they were going to go over the parameters of the assignment, the ground rules and his projected date for getting it done. No more unnecessary retakes, she vowed. At that point, her stomach growled a protest. "And no more missed meals!"

It was dark by the time she rang the doorbell at David's house; she'd had to drive more slowly than usual because of patchy fog. When there was no answer, she knew exactly where to look for him. Picking up her gadget bag, which held her favorite Nikon and the current batch of photographs, she got out of the car and went to the back of the house. He was sitting on the darkened patio, a slumped outline on a wrought-iron bench. She made no attempt to get closer to him than she had the other time. Certain that he was deeply asleep, she called his name softly, not wanting to startle him.

The voice—that husky, honey-sweet voice—played at the blurred edges of his consciousness. It wasn't threatening. He'd heard it almost daily on the telephone, almost nightly in unlikely dreams, just as this was a dream. She wasn't really here. But then he heard the voice again. "David, I need to talk to you." The words floated to him on moisture-saturated air—from not more than twenty feet away.

He sat bolt upright as if galvanized. The voice was no dream! "Karen!" His emotions warred with each other. He fought to suppress pleasure at seeing her again, while fearing what would happen if she saw him. Reason dictated that the sooner she left, the better it would be for both of them. "What are you doing here?" he asked, striving for calm.

"I brought the latest prints."

"You shouldn't have bothered making a special trip. Well, you can leave them on the bench."

"No, I can't. Not this time. We have some things to discuss."

"What was wrong with the telephone?" He had come to enjoy his almost daily conversations with the feisty Karen.

"I felt it was time we got something settled—face-to-face." She could have bitten her tongue as she saw him jerk to attention at her unfortunate choice of words. "I didn't mean—"

"I should have known I couldn't trust you!" he cut in, his eyes straining to see her in the darkness.

"This isn't a matter of trust. I'm not creeping up on you, invading your privacy. I just thought that maybe if we could talk, we might be able to work things out," she said, striving for diplomacy.

"What things?" he snapped.

She stared at his figure through the misty darkness. "All the retakes, for example."

"Just do the shots and don't worry about how many retakes you have to do," he said in a voice that grated.

"When is enough enough?" she asked wearily.

"When I say so!"

"Or when you think that Larson will get tired and say forget the assignment entirely," she said, putting all the jagged pieces together for the first time. *Stupid, naive, credulous fool*, she castigated herself.

"That's not what I had in mind at all," he denied, and heard her laugh shortly in disbelief. "Maybe it's a good thing you did come," he went on. "The assignment isn't working."

"Tell me about it! I've followed your instructions to the letter and wasted time, both mine and the paper's, on this month-long wild-goose chase. It would have saved us all a lot of trouble, and me a lot of future embarrassment, if you'd just said no when I called you on the phone three weeks ago."

"I'm sorry."

"Sorry doesn't quite cut it," she snarled. "I've put in a lot of time and effort, stalled Larson when I had to. This was going to be an important career move for me."

"You'll have other chances."

"Sure, for neighborhood turtle races and dog-and-cat shows. I'll be lucky if Larson doesn't tell me to take a long walk off a short pier."

"I'll call him."

"Big deal! You call him, but I have to face him. Even if this whole charade wasn't designed just to keep Larson off your back, that's the end result, the way I see it. You didn't want this assignment in the first place. And you didn't want to work with me. Well, congratulations. You've accomplished both your goals." She reached for the gadget bag that hung from her shoulder, one hand automatically clutching her Nikon as she removed the envelope she'd brought with her. "Your last batch of photographs." She laughed shortly, stepping forward to toss them at him.

"Don't come any closer," he ordered, retreating toward the patio wall.

"Don't worry, I won't. I always keep my word," she retorted. "You don't hold that much fascination for me. I have no driving compulsion to waste my time with a person who's so full of self-pity."

"You were paid for your time."

"Paid," she echoed. His sarcasm seemed to burn inside her. Seized by anger and frustration, she felt herself trembling from head to foot. Her hands shook so badly that she barely kept a grip on the body of her camera, the primary extension of herself. "Well, since I've been paid, I'll just have to see that you get your money's worth, won't I?" And then, without even trying to steady her grip on the camera—or thinking of the consequences of her actions—she turned toward David Carter's voice in the shadows and snapped the shutter.

"Damn you!" he exclaimed, exerting a massive effort to move across the patio at the same time. The flash had virtually blinded him. "Damn your eyes, you bitch!"

More than once he'd cursed her for interfering in his life. Now he damned her again, because even the silence didn't sound the same anymore. Even when the last vestige of light had faded, the dark quiet was filled with the echo of her presence.

3

WHEN KAREN GOT BACK to the car, her hands were still shaking so badly that she could barely turn the key in the ignition. All the way home, her fingers were fused to the steering wheel in a kind of death grip as her horrified mind replayed the whole ugly scene.

How could she have betrayed his trust? It didn't matter, she realized, that her impulsive action was born of intense frustration and bitter disappointment at his own betrayal of their agreement. She had acted totally out of character. She had allowed anger to direct her actions, wanting above all things to score some point against David—to get back at him in some way because he had struck at her through the most important thing in her life: her work.

She flicked a sidelong glance at the camera she'd used, feeling not triumph, but an emptiness deeper and more painful than anything she'd felt in years. Because for the first and only time in her life, she had used her camera not as a recorder or interpreter of events, but as a weapon, as a means of inflicting pain on another human being. And she had struck at his most vulnerable point: his face.

The next morning she looked unwillingly into her mirror. In the unforgiving harshness of fluorescent light, a zombie looked back at her. She looked terrible and felt worse. Her fair skin was much paler than usual, and dark circles shadowed her eyes. How naive she'd been to think that after conversing with the marvelous Karen Anderson, someone as withdrawn as David Carter would be socialized and ready to work. "How dumb," she groaned aloud.

She put on a pair of well-worn jeans and a comfortable sweatshirt as she prepared to spend the day where she was usually able to be herself, in her darkroom. Karen did free-lance artistic photography, in addition to her assignment work for the *Met*. Since she'd been spending so much time on the David Carter merry-go-round, she had several rolls of film still to be developed, and more than a few contact sheets to scan so that she could work on the actual prints.

By late afternoon her backlog was cleared up, and several prints had been made to her satisfaction. Only one roll of film remained undeveloped, the one still in the camera from the night before. She took the roll of negatives from the camera, tempted for the first time in her life not to expose her work to the light of day. "Coward," she mumbled.

Leaving the film undeveloped wouldn't do her a whole lot of good, she realized. She might not have physical evidence, but her mind certainly hadn't allowed her to forget what had happened. Maybe if she developed the film and made a print of the exposure she'd taken of David Carter, she might be able to exorcise some of the demons that had plagued the previous night's sleep and all her waking moments since.

"You're a professional photographer," she told herself as she began processing the film. "Think of this as any other job." Easier said than done, she realized. She had to work much more slowly than usual; her hands didn't usually shake when she processed film. When the negatives were finally dry, she automatically scanned frame after frame, image after image. And then she came to the last picture on the roll. The picture of David.

Compelled to continue, Karen hurried to develop a positive print. In the bath of development solution, the print was no better, no clearer than the tiny square of negative. Everything was a blur because of the hazy mist of the night before. The light had been all wrong, and the subject had been a moving target. And, she recalled, she hadn't been all that steady when she'd snapped the shutter. She repeated the process, but the next print was no less blurred than the first. She set them both aside.

Now she was finally seeing David Carter as he really was—or at least his outline—frozen in one instant in time. Frozen in darkness. No longer was he a growling voice on a dark night, or a presence at the other end of a phone line, or a smiling face on the cover of *Metro-Lights*. The light from the flash glinted off the crutches; his stance embodied tension. He stood as if poised to run after her, only of course he couldn't do that. She'd broken the cardinal rule—that she would never try to see him. Suddenly it didn't seem to matter that he hadn't kept his side of the bargain. She'd been deliberately cruel as a result of losing her temper. But temper was no excuse.

For a moment Karen's eyes were unfocused on the dim, red-tinted darkness. She could hear the words David had shouted at her last night. "Damn your eyes, you bitch." She shuddered at the thought of the fury hurled at her. His emotions had torn loose, exposing a barely healed wound. It had been the same for her. For the first time since she'd met David— "No, be honest," she ordered herself. *Ever since she'd met David* the dead spot at the center of her being had been coming to life. The photograph itself was a by-product of emotion on both sides. She shook her head as David's invisible pain, his aloneness, touched some place deep within her, maybe the edge of her very soul, where no one and nothing had come close for so long. "I'm sorry, David."

But as she herself had said to him the night before, sorry didn't quite cut it. Not by a long shot. She knew that it wasn't enough to say those words in the company of dryers and developing tanks. She went into the living room, taking the prints with her in shaking hands. Then she took pen and paper, intending to write him a note of apology. But in trying to think of the right words, one repeated itself in her brain like a litany. Sorry.

"Dear David, I'm so sorry that I..." *That I what? That I rushed in where angels, and even your own boss, didn't tread? That I went back on my word about disturbing your privacy?* There was no excuse for that, no matter what the provocation.

An hour later Karen was surrounded by a pile of crumpled failures. Frustrated, she closed her eyes briefly, took a deep breath and started again. When she'd finished she took another look at what she'd written. It wouldn't win a Pulitzer Prize; it might not even be read. But at least it was worth a try.

She hand-copied the note onto a sheet of bond paper, which she put into a stiff envelope along with the print. She had to resist taking the coward's way out and putting the whole thing in the mail. Before she could change her mind she grabbed her keys, not even bothering to slip anything on over her sweatshirt.

She was about halfway there when the skies seemed to open up, the blowing wind and rain threatening to overpower windshield wipers that had long been due for replacement. Her tires slid more than once on the leaf-covered roadway. The weather was a perfect match for her already bleak mood.

Once the Volvo reached the front of David's house, she knew that the longest and hardest part of the trip was yet to come. As she watched the rain come down in sheets, she toyed with the idea of waiting until it let up. She had neither raincoat nor umbrella. But that might take a while, judging from the force of the downpour.

Resignedly she picked up the envelope, wondering how best to keep it dry. She found an empty plastic bag and turned it inside out. Not terrific, but not bad for an emergency, she decided as she prepared to get to David's front door as fast as possible.

She was only ten feet from the house, but by the time she'd covered even that short distance, she was drenched from head to foot, wet, cold and utterly miserable. With one hand she rang the doorbell, shaking her head in a vain attempt to escape the icy rivulets of water that were running down the back of her neck into the loose collar of the sweatshirt and, from there, down between her breasts.

At the sound of the doorbell, David, who was in the kitchen fixing coffee, stilled. He wasn't expecting anyone. The *Met* courier had already made a delivery. As the bell sounded again, he slid his muscular forearms into the cuffs of the crutches and made his way to the living-room window.

Incredibly, standing in the pouring rain, was Karen Anderson, wearing no protective gear and looking thoroughly soaked. The cap she usually wore was missing, and her hair was half pinned up, half coming down in limp tendrils.

"What do you want?" he growled, opening the door a crack. "Yesterday was enough. I don't want or need an encore. So just go back downtown and crawl under your rock!"

"I didn't come here for an encore," she responded, too tired to reply in kind to his sarcasm.

"So why are you here?" he rasped.

"I have something for you."

"I don't want or need *anything* from you."

"Please take it," she urged. "Just let me hand it to you."

She looked for all the world as if she were planted. Maybe she wouldn't move until she flowered, like some kind of blond-haired tree. "All right," he snapped impatiently, opening the door a scant six inches farther and extending his hand. "Let's have it, whatever it is. I'll get to it later."

She handed him the drenched plastic bag and its contents. "I'll stay here while you read it."

"Go back to your car," he told her gruffly.

"I can't get any wetter." Maybe if he knew she was standing there he'd be more likely to read what she'd written. And maybe the slight overhang from the roof would help protect her from wind and rain.

"Suit yourself," he replied, slamming the door decisively in Karen's very wet face. At that point, he didn't much care if she stood on his doorstep in the rain or drove back to the city, he told himself as he discarded the wet plastic bag, then tossed the stiff brown envelope onto the glass-topped coffee table in the living room. Deliberately he looked away from the envelope, fully intending to ignore it. He hesitated, but not for long. His innate curiosity and the unrelenting reminder of the waiting figure on the other side of his front door overcame his reluctance.

Releasing the crutches, David sat down heavily on the sofa, reaching for the packet. The overprinting on the outside included the *Met*'s familiar logo and the legend, Photographs—Do Not Bend! *I bet I'm going to love her eight-by-ten glossies of the beast in the garden*, he told himself bitterly as he remembered the night before. He opened the envelope gingerly, sliding its contents onto the table in front of him. And stared.

There was one photograph, a silhouette of himself near the wrought-iron bench. The flash had evidently supplied only enough light to outline his body. He saw no details, only a dark blur. "That must have disappointed our little photographer," he muttered. Accompanying the photograph was a letter, written in small, neat pen strokes.

David,
You may wonder at the lack of detail in the photograph. I am not a bad photographer, despite the conclusions you may have drawn from the work I've done for you, and from the picture I took without permission last night when temper overcame my better judgement. When I first sat down to write this note, I was simply going to say, "I know you can't forgive me, but I'm sorry for intruding on your privacy in so graphic a way." Well, I've changed my mind. I'm not sorry. I'm glad.

"Well, *hell*! I don't believe I'm reading this," he muttered, more than half tempted to rip the paper and the print into several dozen shreds. But something—journalistic curiosity—got the better of him for the second time that night, and with renewed determination he turned his attention to the rest of the note.

> You see, David, in taking and developing the picture, I learned something about you, something I'd like to share. The camera, like the eye, records only what it sees. Last night, it saw a man, or rather, the shadow of a man. And, as in real life, the image shows no detail, no clarity, no feeling, and no light. In place of flesh and blood there is only emptiness, bitterness and darkness. This is what I see reflected from you, even though I have never really seen you. If people turn away from you, as you say they do, are they avoiding you—or the emptiness that looks out from your eyes?
>
> Karen Anderson

David shook his head as if to clear it, leaning back against the sofa with mixed feelings of shock and bewilderment. Of all the things he might have expected to receive from Karen Anderson—insults, condemnation, pleas to continue the assignment, perhaps—a shadow-portrait and a near-poetic homily on his way of life were certainly furthest from his mind. He picked up the photograph again and looked at it. And wondered if she'd really meant what she'd said about waiting to leave until she was sure he'd read the letter. Because, if so, there would be one very wet lady outside his front door.

He opened the door slightly, then spoke her name. There *was* one very wet lady outside his front door.

"Did you look in the envelope?" she asked, not turning her head toward the sound of his voice.

"Yes," he replied, still partially in a daze. And then he knew that he had to talk to her. *Had to.* "Will you come inside?"

"No, thank you," she replied as formally as she could, considering that her teeth were chattering. "I just wanted you to look at the photograph and see what I'd written. I won't bother you anymore. I'll see Larson tomorrow." She wrapped her arms around herself in a futile attempt to capture some warmth, then turned back to her car.

"Karen," he called again, "please come in. I mean it. I'd like to talk to you."

She thought the storm must be playing tricks with her hearing. From this distance it sounded as if he really did want her to come inside. She hesitated, then shrugged fatalistically, turning toward the door he was holding open for her. She walked with her head turned away from him.

As she walked past him into his house, Karen kept her curiosity in check. All she could see of David was a pair of clenched hands, his fingers wrapped around the horizontal grips of the cuffed metal crutches. She felt like a Christian thrown to a particularly hungry lion as she waited for the explosion that didn't come. Her teeth chattered no matter how tightly she clenched her jaw, and she shivered uncontrollably from an enervating combination of cold, wetness and nervousness.

Eyes narrowed, David watched Karen's slow progress into his house, realizing that she was the first woman—the first person—he'd really seen in more than a year. She kept her face averted from him, but there was no concealing her womanly form from his eyes. She wasn't tall, certainly not much more than five-foot-five. Her sweatshirt and jeans clung to her like a second skin, outlining her high, firm breasts, the gentle swell of her hips and her long, slender legs.

She stood shivering before him, as water dripped continuously from the skeins of dark blond hair that streamed back from her face. He still didn't know what she really looked like, he thought absently. He felt something stirring deep inside as he discovered with a very real sense of shock that he wanted nothing more than to take her into his arms and make her warm again. Gritting his teeth, he ruthlessly suppressed the impulse. "There's a bathroom down the hall from the living room."

"I—I don't understand. . . ." She hesitated, not moving from her place just inside the door.

David saw her small hands clench and unclench at her sides. She probably thought he was going to tell her to go to hell for a change. "From where I'm standing, it looks like you're wet to the skin."

"Very perceptive," she muttered.

"You've got to get dried off or you'll get sick," he said quietly.

What do you care if I get sick, came the morose thought. "All right. I'll go and dry off," she responded dully.

"You're too wet to just dry off. I don't want your pneumonia on my conscience. Go and take a hot shower. You'll find everything you need. There's a robe, hot towels and a hair dryer in the cabinet," he said matter-of-factly. "After you're finished, you can put your clothes in the dryer. The laundry room is right off the kitchen."

"David, you don't have to do this."

"No, but I want to," he said without hesitation. "Go on. Take your shower. And then we'll talk about that special-delivery letter you just gave me. Unless you're afraid to stay and talk to me for a while?" he queried silkily.

"It won't take me long," she informed him stiffly.

"Take your time. When you get through you'll find coffee and a mug on the kitchen counter. And I'll be in the living room."

Almost too cold and exhausted to function, Karen luxuriated in the pulsating hot shower and in the warmth that came from the heated towels and robe she found on a freestanding rack. But afterward, as she drew the chocolate-brown robe around her, she experienced an odd feeling. This was David's robe; he wore it. And since it had come from the electrically heated towel rack, she could almost imagine that the delicious warmth permeating her from neck to ankles was actually the heat from his own body.

In spite of the physical warmth, Karen shuddered at the thought. It had been such a long time since she'd been in a man's arms. And surely, if she ever did seek the refuge of a man's embrace again, that man would not be David Carter! She knew very well that she would never be allowed to get close enough to him to find out what the warmth of his body felt like. As if that mattered, she told herself, consciously stiffening her spine and squaring her shoulders. She'd managed to survive without the solace of male-female intimacy.

After drying her hair and combing it into a semblance of order, Karen surveyed her clothes. Everything was drenched except for her bikini panties, which she slipped on under the robe. The other things she gathered up and put into the dryer in the laundry room before pouring herself a mug of hot coffee. Then there was nothing else to do except make her way once more into the living room.

After making sure that the fixings for coffee were ready and waiting, David had kindled the fire that now cast a warm brightness over the living room. Then he'd eased himself down onto the sofa that was usually a source of comfort for his often tired muscles and stared blindly into the flames. Over the crackle of newly burning wood, he had listened to Karen's progress—the rush of water into the bathtub, the hard-driving force of the shower and, finally, the whir of the hair dryer.

For once the warmth of the blaze in the fireplace failed to cheer him. The tension within him increased until all he wanted was for the waiting to be over. And in spite of that, calling himself a rank coward, he leaned toward the three-way lamp that lit the room, turning it down to its lowest setting. Now he heard her start the clothes dryer, pour coffee. Soon she would be back in the living room. He waited for the inevitable.

It was with a growing sense of anticlimax that David watched Karen, barefoot and enveloped in his own robe, walk slowly, gracefully into the living room. She held a mug of coffee in one hand, while the other lifted the hem of the robe, which was far too long for her. Her hair hung forward, much lighter now that it was partially dried. She took a seat in the armchair in front of the fireplace, deliberately turning away from him and toward the bookshelves that lined that corner of the room. It was painfully obvious, he realized with a stunning sense of disappointment, that in spite of the brave words in her letter, even Karen wasn't courageous enough to look him in the face!

Karen had no idea how long she sat there, sipping hot, black coffee. Warmth emanated from the fireplace, drawing her like a magnet but doing little to thaw the ice that remained lodged deep inside her. The only sounds in the room came from the crackling wood. *Say something!* she pleaded silently to her clearly unwilling host. The moments went by. Her coffee cup was nearly empty. And still he said nothing. Finally she couldn't stand it anymore, yet she didn't know where to begin. *At the beginning,* she thought. *Pretend you're a guest in someone's house—you are! Remember the manners your mother drilled into you.*

"Thank you for allowing me to get warm and dry," she said huskily. "I must look like the Wreck of the Hesperus."

She was curled up in the chair, her hair fluffed into a golden curtain as it fanned over her shoulders like a shawl. He could barely see her face, but he could see the curves of her body and the way they were outlined by the rough texture of the robe. His robe. "Sure," he managed, talking to her unseen profile, almost adding, *any time.*

At the sound of his voice, Karen found she was barely able to restrain herself from glancing in his direction. "You make good coffee."

"Mr. Coffee," he informed her curtly. "Karen, did you really mean what you said in your letter?"

"I always mean what I say."

"I find that hard to believe."

"Look, my prose may not be up to your journalistic standards, but every word I wrote was the truth!"

"You're just as afraid of what you'll see as anyone else, or you wouldn't be cowering in that corner with your eyes glued to a collection of books, as if you meant to catalogue them!"

"You're forgetting something," she reminded him. "I promised that I wouldn't look at you until you requested it. Last night, my camera saw you because I lost my temper. I'm sorry for that—for losing my temper, I mean. But I'm not sorry that I took the picture. And everything that I said in my note still goes!" With that, she forced herself to take a healthy swallow of nearly cold coffee.

Almost without realizing it, David reached out and turned the light switch up. All the way. Then, with a deep, steadying breath, he invited softly, "Please. Look at me, Karen."

4

VERY CAREFULLY she set the cup down on the fireplace. Her heart faltered briefly, then began beating relentlessly. She took a deep breath, hoping that she wouldn't react as others had, by turning away, by hurting him even more than he'd been hurt already. She turned, slowly, until she was face to face with the man himself.

Her grip tightened convulsively on the arms of the chair as her gaze swept the features of the man who sat still, unmoving, across the room from her. From the way he'd spoken, she'd expected to see a face that was a flawed, carved mask. She felt her grip relax imperceptibly as the reality began to sink in. The scars served to outline a face that might not be good-looking in the conventional way, but that was at once arrestingly, intensely masculine.

He was the same man whose picture she'd seen on the cover of *Metro-Lights*. And yet, he wasn't. The man in the photograph had been smiling, standing straight, tall and, above all, confident. That confidence had long since been eroded by the shock of physical wounds whose aftereffects she could see, and the pain of emotional and psychological hurts that were, perhaps, even worse. Ready humor and love of life had been erased, to be replaced by wariness, distrust and deep-rooted cynicism. All of that was reflected in the ramrod stiffness of his body, the clenched fists and the tautly controlled muscles of his face.

His strong features were now outlined by the jagged ridge of scar tissue that scored his left cheek and temple. The scar on his cheek etched a vertical furrow that emphasized the lean planes of his face. The one on his temple disappeared into the fullness of his dark brown hair. But the most arresting aspect of his face was not the scars, but the piercing, brilliantly blue eyes that stared unblinking, hopeless and hauntingly trapped from his tanned skin.

Very deliberately she explored the rest of him, automatically noting the curling brown hair that protruded from the open-necked cream shirt that outlined broad shoulders and muscular arms. She saw the knit fabric grow taut with each expansion of his chest as he breathed unevenly. Cuffed metal crutches rested against the sofa, within easy reach of hands that were bunched into fists on either side of his legs. He was wearing tan cords that emphasized his powerful thighs. A muscle worked in his clenched jaw as if he were bracing himself for a body blow. And she knew with regret that she was the cause of this terrible tension. He expected the blow to come from her.

Feelings crowded forward in a jumble, waiting to be named. But the most profound of all was a sense of anticlimax. Because of the way David himself had spoken, he'd clearly expected her to be repelled. In fact, he didn't look nearly as bad as he'd led her to believe—as he believed himself to look, she realized.

Instead, she was shocked by the fact that not only was she not repelled by him, she was actually drawn to his looks—and to him—as if by an invisible string. She had been emotionally isolated for so long that these new feelings rocked her, leaving her more than a little shaky and off-balance. As for rejection, revulsion or fear, all of which he'd plainly expected, there was none. Karen simply didn't feel those things in relation to David. And never would.

David sat ramrod-straight, enduring the scrutiny he himself had invited, wondering when it would end. He felt for all the world as if he were a prisoner in the dock, waiting for the jury to come in with a verdict. And expecting to hear the word "guilty." He couldn't have moved if he'd wanted to, waiting tensely as her practiced, photographer's eyes observed the details of his body. As he endured her examination, his mouth too dry to swallow, he began a survey of his own, proud that he could come up with the inner strength to focus his gaze on the woman across the room from him. This was no street urchin, he told himself, his heart quickening as he watched the play of firelight over the piquantly lovely oval of her face.

His quick reporter's mind caught hold of something like a puzzle. How often did a beautiful woman go to such extraordinary lengths to conceal her own loveliness? And why? Once upon a time, he might have taken it upon himself to find out. Once. Not now. For Karen Anderson was his first—and last—house guest, one who had set herself up as judge, jury and intruder. He could almost feel her touch as her glance flickered over the scars that showed. Why did he have the uncanny feeling that she was also seeing the scars that were hidden in his soul? "Karen..." he began hesitantly, unable to bear the waiting any longer.

Given what David really looked like, the words in her note had been prophetic, Karen realized. Emptiness did look out from those blue eyes. His real injuries were not the scars on his face and the weakened muscles in his legs. The real hurts were inside, where they couldn't be reached. Deep inside. Emotional pain. The kind of pain she herself knew about. Pain that seared so deeply that the wound never had a chance to heal.

What was the cure for the kind of pain that he suffered? she wondered bleakly. Gone was the man of action, the dynamic reporter. What was missing in David Carter no amount of surgery could ever replace. He'd lost more than good looks and mobility in that Middle Eastern hellhole. He had lost himself.

Karen had been looking through cameras for far too long not to be able to read faces. And David's face was far too easy to read. There was fear, anxiety and, on another level, a deep-seated need for approval that he felt would never be given. Instinctively she knew that he wouldn't believe her if she simply told him the truth, that his injuries probably seemed far worse to him than they did to the world around him. The words were already in her note.

She didn't bother to ask herself why she was being so unusually hesitant. Instead, she inched forward in her chair, feeling as if she were invading his territory. And asked him very softly, "Does it hurt?"

"Does it—" Shock reverberated through him as Karen's response made him feel as if he'd been plunged naked into ice-cold water. "No one has ever thought to ask," he replied almost to himself, his voice barely audible.

"That's not strictly true, David. After all, by your own admission, no one has gotten close enough to ask you anything for quite a long time."

"Touché," David replied, the fingers of one hand briefly tracing the pattern of scar tissue on his cheek. "There was a lot of pain at first, in my face and my legs. My back, too. I feel echoes of it when I get overtired, even now. The damp Maryland weather doesn't do a whole lot for me, either." He saw her open her mouth, as if to say something, then sink back into the chair as if she'd thought better of it. "What, Karen?" he asked softly.

"The crutches—" She broke off. "Never mind," she said with a sigh, shaking her head.

"My legs don't work very well. At this point, I'm not strong enough to do without the crutches for very long."

"At this point?" she interrupted gently.

"Let's put it this way: if I didn't use them, I sure wouldn't get very far," he concluded, absently rubbing his right leg.

She noticed the gesture, and the drawn look on his face, and wondered if he was feeling some of those echoes of pain he'd talked about. "The doctors—what do they say?"

"The orthopedic surgeons say they've gone about as far with me as they can go. I was in physical therapy for a while."

"But not now."

David shook his head. "They set up a program that I can follow at home. I've got some equipment, and I work to build on my strengths and maintain the physical level I've achieved. With some luck, I might even go beyond it."

"What does that mean?" she asked, suppressed excitement threading through her voice.

"If I really work at it, I might just graduate to a cane someday," he told her, a wry smile pulling at the corner of his mouth.

At that she caught her breath, mentally crossing her fingers for him.

"As far as my face is concerned," he was saying, "plastic surgery has helped some. But I was away from good medical care for too long after—after the incident. And aside from that, the kind of skin I have doesn't respond well to current techniques. They say maybe in a few years. Who knows?" He shrugged, staring into the flames. "I—" He broke off, shaking his head.

She wanted to tell him that he needn't worry about putting himself through the pain of further surgery. She liked his face the way it was, scars and all. In fact, the scars gave him a unique, rough-hewn quality. She said nothing, however, unwilling to disrupt the fragile truce that seemed to be linking them. More than that, she was afraid he wouldn't believe her.

The tension, the solidified ache that was evident in the rigidity of his posture, drew her like a magnet. And yielding to an impulse that she was unable to analyze, she padded silently across the floor and sat down beside him on the sofa. "Don't tell me any more if it's too painful for you."

David opened his mouth to speak but closed it again, saying nothing, momentarily overcome by her presence next to him. One part of his mind was busy recording details—the way her nearly dry hair was curling into waves. At first it had almost looked light brown. Now, when dry, it was the shade of natural honey, the leaping flames turning it molten gold. He had to restrain himself from reaching out and touching it.

He became aware of the delicate perfume she wore, then realized that it was no bottled essence, but the fragrance of his soap and shampoo, combined with her own elusive scent. Her skin had an opalescent glow in the brightness of the firelight. And she was near enough that he could clearly see how the fabric of his own robe seemed to caress the slender length of her throat and drape itself over the tender curves of her breasts. She was near enough to touch. He kept his hands clasped tightly on his knees.

He drew a deep breath, shaking his head. "It's not that it's painful for me to talk about what happened to me. It's not that I don't accept the way I am. I do. I don't have a choice. And I know my physical limitations. But I can't stop remembering the way I was," he said, his voice barely above a whisper. "It's bad enough remembering what it was like to be a gymnast in college, or to run in the *Met*'s 10K marathon. What's even worse is the fact that this—" his fingers brushed his face, then bit into the muscles of one thigh "—this keeps me tied down, away from the important things in my life, from the kind of work I want to do. I hate it!"

"Is that why you decided to live out here alone? What about your family and friends?" Karen asked, his openness giving her the courage to voice the question she'd wanted so badly to ask that first night in the garden.

"Family!" He laughed harshly. "My parents aren't a factor in my life. They've never approved of my choice of career, and they couldn't quite manage to look me in the face without flinching when I came back. I haven't seen them in more than a year. As far as I know, my father's main focus is still his clothing business—he's a senior partner. My mother has always been involved with various corporations and foundations. As for friends—well, after what happened with the lady I was dating before I left the States, I decided I'd had enough."

"What happened?" Karen asked unwillingly, recalling Mickie Lewin's harsh words about the last woman in David's life.

"You have to ask?" he retorted, bitterness coloring his voice. "Eleanor could barely stand to be in the same room with me. Oh, she tried to hide her feelings, but I knew it would never be the same between us. She left Baltimore when I was still in the hospital."

When he paused, a faraway look in his eyes, Karen tried to control the surge of anger she felt against his family, and the woman he'd loved. She wanted to say that the scars had probably been raw-looking when he'd first come home. She wanted to tell him that his lack of mobility shouldn't have made any difference— not if the people around him had really cared. But before she could get the words out, he was speaking again, his voice low and bitter.

"Hell, I don't blame her. When we started dating, she had the travel beat. I was just getting ready to go to the Middle East. The first year we were together, everything fit together just fine. We met every six or eight weeks or so in Paris—or London or Rome."

Reading between the lines, Karen could hear what David wasn't saying: the woman had been attracted to him because of his glamorous life-style. The life-style that he missed, as well. When it had been lost, there'd been nothing to tie them together. If the woman had waited, Karen mused, David would have healed, and they could have been together. Hell, the woman might even have helped his healing process. But she couldn't stop long enough to get off her merry-go-round, Karen thought in disgust. "Her loss, David."

He slanted her a sidelong glance. "Yeah, well, she hadn't signed on for a relationship with an invalid.

Hanging around, waiting for me to graduate from being flat on my back to a wheelchair to crutches would really have cramped her style. And can you imagine any woman wanting to wake up next to this?" he ground out, one hand brushing the scarred side of his face.

"*I* would!" she blurted out.

David looked her up and down in disbelief. She looked mad enough to spit, he thought with dark amusement as he saw her fingers clutch the edges of the robe. And then his gaze zeroed in on the slender hand nearest to him—her left hand—the hand whose third finger bore a bright gold band. Karen Anderson was married, he realized with a peculiar sense of shock. What would her husband think if he knew she was sitting practically naked next to another man? "Yes, well, we won't have to put that to the test, will we, seeing as how you're spoken for," he drawled, not bothering to mask the sarcasm in his voice.

His cynical words poured salt onto a wound that had never quite closed. "You don't know what you're talking about," Karen countered, continuing doggedly as if he hadn't spoken, knowing only that she had to get the words out before they choked her. "If the man I loved—" Here, her voice broke, and she had to swallow hard before she could go on. "If the man I loved was scarred—or unable to walk—or both—it wouldn't faze me. Not one little bit."

David surveyed the woman next to him and saw a walking-wounded look in her tear-bright green eyes. He had seen the same look in his own mirror. She was turning the wedding ring round and round on her finger. "The man you love . . ." he prodded softly.

"My husband," she inserted automatically.

"Your husband is very lucky, Karen," he said, not at all prepared for the pain that lanced through him as he said the words.

Karen turned to David, hardly seeing him, because her eyes were filled with tears that threatened to overflow. "You're much luckier than my husband," she managed through clenched teeth.

"How can you say that?" he demanded, wondering at the sheen of tears in her eyes and the tremor of her lovely mouth.

"My husband—is dead."

Four words. And they said it all. Damn. Impulsively he grasped her hands, which he found ice-cold. "I'm so sorry," he whispered, his voice rough.

Her instinct was to draw away from him, back into the protective shell she had created so long ago as a shield against the pain. But some overriding instinct told her that to do so would hurt David, who hadn't reached out to anyone for so long. So she held herself stiffly, carefully, trying to concentrate on not breaking down completely and making a fool of herself. And she let her fingers rest in the warm strength of his callused hands.

He looked down at their clasped hands, much shaken by the contrast between them. Her slender fingers curled inside his as trustingly as if they were small birds come home to roost. The bones of her wrists were delicate. There was an overall air of fragility about her. But somewhere inside Karen there was also a core of forged steel, something that had enabled her to face terrible tragedy and keep on going.

Karen looked at David's bent head, and yielded to an uncontrollable impulse to comfort, to ease his pain. She slid one hand from his grasp, reaching up to gently stroke his scarred cheek. "Your scars—they look much worse to you than they do to me," she whispered. He tensed beside her, then shook his head in disbelief, his lips barely brushing her palm. The feather-light touch electrified her, forging an almost physical link.

A raucous sound shattered the poignant mood.

"The dryer," David said hoarsely.

She eased her other hand from his. "I'd better get dressed now." His touch had warmed her; now, in its absence, she had to suppress a shiver. She had no reason to stay in David's house any longer.

She couldn't wait to leave, he realized as she went to the laundry room and came back minutes later in the creased but dry clothes she'd worn earlier.

"I usually get to work at eight-thirty in the morning," Karen said, feeling awkward as she stood and looked down at him. "I'll see Mr. Larson as soon as I get in. By eight-thirty-one, it should be all over," she said with a wry attempt at humor.

"I'm sorry for everything, Karen. I really am. I wish things could have been different." If things had been different, he would have welcomed the chance to work with her. Hell, he would have given anything just to part the robe—to see what the mirror in his bathroom had seen when Karen had undressed. She affected him as no woman ever had, and that included Eleanor. But wishing didn't make it so; he'd found that out long ago. "I'll see you to the door."

Her green eyes followed each methodical movement he made as he swung easily to his feet. Until now she'd only seen him sitting down. Standing, he was several inches over six feet tall; he towered over her own five-feet-four inches. For a timeless instant she was reminded of the *Metro-Lights* photograph. She hadn't known that David Carter, but what she couldn't understand was the twisting pain of regret because she would never really get to know the enigmatic man who now stood beside her.

"I'll call Larson first thing in the morning," David said as he moved across the living room with her.

Karen nodded, her steps automatically slowing to keep pace with him.

"And Karen—what happened is my fault. Not yours. You won't have to take the heat for this fiasco, I promise. It won't reflect on you."

She didn't answer. She couldn't. For some reason her throat had tightened, and she had to concentrate to get it working again.

"Karen?"

"Thanks," she managed finally. "I appreciate that. Goodbye, David. And good luck," she added, her voice strained.

"Drive carefully," he called after her, flicking on the outside lights. He closed the door, locking it behind her, then stood by the glass panel and watched her car disappear down the drive.

LATER THAT NIGHT, long after Karen had gone, the memory of her caused sweat to break out on his skin. His mind wouldn't let her leave, and it wouldn't let him rest. Imprinted on his senses were the graceful sway of her body when she walked, the sound of her voice, her scent as she had sat next to him on the sofa, the feel of her slim, capable hands in his own. And the way—for a too-brief instant in time—she had touched his face. His throat tightened at the memory.

He went to the bathroom for a glass of cold water, and she was there, too. The robe she'd worn, his robe, now hung limply on the back of the bathroom door. And he found a strand of golden hair entwined in the teeth of the comb she'd used. He picked it up, removing the hair, as if that action would make her disappear from his mind, as well.

He gave up on the idea of trying to free himself from her presence. On other sleepless nights he'd taken to his typewriter or poured himself a glass of Scotch. Tonight, however, he sat down on the sofa and reread yet another remnant of Karen: her note. He could toss the note and the photograph into the fireplace, but somehow he knew even those actions wouldn't erase her from his memory.

Nothing was the same anymore. She'd gotten under his skin, stripped off his facade, letting in the outside. Shaking his head, he made his way to his office and pulled out a ruled legal pad and a pen, drawing a line down the middle of the page. At the top of one side he wrote, Column A. The other side he labeled Column B. Column A was subtitled Status Quo; Column B read, Do the Assignment.

If he didn't do the project, things would stay as they were, as they had been for so very long. Karen wouldn't come back to bother him. He was certain of that from the way she'd looked and spoken when she'd said goodbye. And after all, he hadn't exactly put himself out to make her feel welcome. If things remained unchanged, he wouldn't have to risk meeting people, wouldn't have to worry about the future, about facing ridicule. He could ignore all the intangible, meaningless fears that crowded his dreams and plagued his waking hours. Everything would stay the same. He would remain invisible.

If he did the project, it would be tantamount to returning to work. Eventually he would have to face the
stares of his colleagues, the people who had known him
before. His old I.D. wouldn't even get him past the paper's security guard. God knew, there was no earthly
resemblance between then and now. If he went back to
work, he'd really have to start using his mind again, and
it would be harder to get the same kind of stories he'd
managed to cover before. What he couldn't deny was
that if he went back, he'd be working with Karen
Anderson, face-to-face. He had to admit how much
that excited him.

If he went back . . .

David stared long and hard at the pad. One from
Column A, one from Column B, just like a menu in a
Chinese restaurant. He shook his head tiredly, annoyed at his own indecision. The work Larson was de-
manding could be a testing ground for him and the
paper, David reasoned. Maybe they wouldn't like his
reporting style any longer. Maybe too many people in
the community or in the workplace would turn away
from him. Maybe he just wouldn't be able to cut it, in-
tellectually or physically. Maybe he was just too
damned scared. But if he didn't do something soon,
what was left of his mental and physical strength would
atrophy, and he would drown in an ocean of slimy
"what ifs?"

Wearily he made his way to the bedroom, where,
tired as he was, sleep still didn't come. Which was
nothing unusual, since he knew that some of his sleep-
lessness was the result of too much tension that day. Too
much tension since Karen Anderson had stormed into

his life. But instead of dreams about people dying around him, and being a target for a Jeep turned into flying shrapnel fragments, his dreams revolved around something—someone—else.

5

KAREN STOOD POISED on the threshold of Glen Larson's office at eight-thirty the next morning.

"You can go in," his secretary, Joan Hart, told her. "But be prepared. He's loaded for bear. I think we were scooped by *The Washington Post*. Again."

Karen shrugged, edging toward the managing editor's office.

"Where the hell were you this morning, anyway?" he was roaring into the telephone. "Why do you think we have a bureau in Washington—for our health?" And then, in a voice that was deadly quiet by contrast, "I'm not like some managing editors you may have heard of. I don't take you out to breakfast when I give you your walking papers. You'll get a one-line memo. Now get your act in gear!

"Dammit!" he muttered as he hung up, strong teeth clamped around the well-worn stem of a meerschaum pipe. And then he looked up at Karen Anderson hovering in the doorway and gestured for her to come inside. "Sit."

She sat, her hands clenched in her lap. Waiting.

"I'm supposed to give you this before we talk," Larson said as he slid a piece of paper across the desk to Karen.

She wondered if it was a one-line memo. She scanned the sheet, then shifted her attention back to him, her eyes wide. "This is a bibliography!"

"I'm impressed," Larson drawled. "I see you went to college. Carter wants you to bring this stuff out to his place by tonight."

So much for David calling up and "explaining" things to Larson. She had to restrain herself from asking, "Why am I bothering to go through all this? It's all a sham!"

"Oh, and tell Carter that the next time he wants books, he should take it up with you or Mickie Lewin. I've got better things to do than play messenger."

Like fry unfortunate reporters. "I'll be sure to tell him when I see him again."

Larson sat up straight in his chair. "You *saw* him!" he echoed, startled. "How did he look?"

"Like someone who'd been badly injured when his Jeep exploded," she replied shortly, almost forgetting who she was talking to.

"And the assignment?"

She looked down at the list of books and had to restrain herself from shredding it. "We're, er, working on it."

"I'll just bet you are." Larson chuckled, apparent approval gleaming in his eyes. "By the way, Ms Miracle Worker, can I expect some copy any time soon?" he asked with deceptive gentleness. "The publisher would like to have a vague idea when this stuff will see daylight."

Karen swallowed, wondering what to say. "I leave that part of the assignment to David."

"Yeah, well, light some fires. Tell him I said to get a move on! Now what was it you wanted to talk to me about this morning?"

"Oh, just wanted to give you a progress report," she said, crossing her fingers against the lie.

"Well, I can see you're working hard on it."

"You can?"

"Yeah. You look like you've been working through the night. Take it easy."

"I'll do that." Oh, right. She couldn't tell Larson that her sleepless night had been the result of her face-to-face meetings with David—both in person, and later, in her dreams. She'd fallen asleep with her face pressed to the palm David's lips had brushed; she'd awakened to a pillow wet with tears. Now she tried to avoid gritting her teeth as she stuffed the bibliography into a side pocket of her jacket and stalked to the *Met* library.

So much for honesty and integrity on David Carter's part, she fumed. He was still bent on pulling the wool over Larson's eyes. And she was still the go-between doomed to miss meals, to be a messenger and waste a lot of time. She couldn't tell Larson what to do, but she'd be damned if she was going to keep taking it from David.

"Doing Carter's legwork?" Mickie Lewin quipped as she handed Karen several books she'd pulled for her.

"I'll try to pretend I didn't hear you say that!"

"How's it going?"

"Let's just say that it's—different. Thanks for having the books ready and waiting." Karen spent the rest of the day lugging around sacks of books and photocopies, playing on librarians' sympathies so that they would allow short-term loans of books that usually never circulated at all. She concentrated on getting everything on the list, and maybe getting David Carter out of her hair once and for all. She barely took the time to hurry through a cup of yogurt for lunch.

By five o'clock she was finally on her way to the Worthington Valley. "Oh, what I wouldn't give for a hot pastrami sandwich!" she moaned. Automatically her fingers searched for the bag of trail mix on the seat beside her. Then she remembered. The trail mix was long gone; she'd used the bag for the photograph the night before. "Damn!"

Karen arrived at his house after seven o'clock, seeing the place clearly for the first time. It was a smallish, brick ranch house with an attached garage. Maybe David had an adapted car, one that allowed him to drive without taxing his legs. Then she dismissed that thought. Why would he have a car when he so clearly had no place to go?

Given David's mercurial personality, Karen had no way of knowing if he would even let her in. And when she rang the doorbell several times and there was no answer, she knew a strong sense of déjà vu. "Here we go again." She laughed without humor, strongly tempted to dump everything on his doorstep, but there was no way she was leaving a pile of expensive books out in the open air with no security.

She expected to find him on the patio; it was deserted. All she saw was an expanse of fieldstone and several benches. She went to the glass sliding door, too intent on her goal to notice the profusion of flowers that surrounded the patio on all sides. When she tried the door, she found it unlocked. Without hesitation she walked inside, calling David's name. And received no response.

Where was he, Karen wondered. Why didn't he hear when she called? Determined to find out, she began to search for him. The patio door had led into the kitchen. From there she went to the empty living room, where she deposited the books and other materials on the coffee table. Retracing her steps of the night before, she rapped on the bathroom door. Nothing. Farther down the hallway, she found a room with a desk, a filing cabinet and a massive electronic typewriter. David's office. Everything was neat and orderly. And silent.

The door to the next room was closed, but she opened it, anyway. She saw a cushioned exercise mat and an assortment of gleaming equipment. There was a universal machine, an exercise bike, a slant board and what looked like a rowing machine. She shook her head, recalling what David had said about being an athlete before his injuries had brought all that to an end.

She felt a rush of heat as she made her way toward the only place she hadn't yet tried, the bedroom. Maybe he slept during the day, she reasoned as she crept toward the last room on the hall. How would he react to someone watching while he slept?

She needn't have worried. She stared at the empty room, a sinking feeling in her breast. A king-size bed was covered with a caramel-colored comforter. There was a dresser, an armoire and a pair of night tables. But no occupant. No David Carter. The annoyance Karen had felt at being sent on yet another fool's errand was quickly replaced by a rush of fear. Where *was* he? By his own admission, he went nowhere and saw no one. It was hardly likely that he'd gone traipsing off. And if he had, he could easily have fallen, or be lying injured somewhere, with no one to know or care.

Karen wanted to do something but had no idea what. Maybe he was out walking, after all. Maybe she could follow him; he couldn't move very fast, after all. And if—when—she found him, at least she'd be able to tell him the books were waiting for him. But then, before she could do that, she noticed yet one more door. At first glance she had assumed it led to a clothes closet.

Or perhaps it was the inside door to the garage. If he was in there, that might explain why he hadn't heard the doorbell or her calling his name.

She turned the handle, pushed the door inward and was struck by a blast of warm, chlorinated air. Her startled eyes quickly took in the long, narrow pool that occupied almost all of the space in the "garage." Next to the pool was a bench, over which were draped several towels, along with the chocolate-brown bathrobe she'd worn the night before. Leaning against the bench were the crutches. And swimming toward the far end of the pool was David, whose powerful shoulders and arms propelled him easily and smoothly through the water.

David reached the end of the pool, then paused briefly, his chest, back and shoulder muscles all feeling the effects of his workout. It was time to get out, he realized as he felt a chill. He didn't want cramp, even in a lap pool that was one-half regulation size. He turned, intending to swim to the bench side of the pool, but stopped, wondering if his chlorinated eyes were making him see a mirage. Because there in the doorway, big as life, was Karen Anderson, standing as still as a statue.

He dashed a hand across his face, brushing aside the hair that obscured his eyes. "Hi," he called.

"Hi, yourself."

The mirage was as real as he was. "Come on in. You're letting out all the warm air."

She did as he asked, closing the door gently behind her. She could see that he exuded vitality, from the top of his water-slicked, sable-dark hair to the broad shoulders and arms that supported him as he braced himself at the opposite side of the pool. "I thought you were going to square things with Larson?" she asked pointedly.

"Yeah, well, I wanted to talk to you about that."

"No more, David," she pleaded tiredly. "Look, I just wanted to tell you that I got you the books Larson said you needed, although I can't imagine what you need them for. Happy reading," she concluded, preparing to leave.

"Wait a minute."

"Why?" she asked bluntly.

"Because I really would like to talk to you, that's why," he said patiently, fully aware that he was going to have an uphill fight in winning her trust.

"I'm listening," she told him impatiently.

"And I'm cold."

"Oh. Well. Why don't you get out of the pool? Do you have to stay in a certain time?"

"I try to do thirty full laps each session; a lap is twice the length of this pool. I didn't quite make it today. The air cooled down."

"I'm sorry," she said stiffly, not about to tell him she'd invaded his privacy solely because she was worried about him, and for no other reason.

"I'm not," he said to her great surprise. "I was working and got a late start on the session. And I do want to talk to you as soon as I get out of here."

She saw the ripple of glistening muscles as he shivered, clinging to the side of the pool, and wondered if he was too embarrassed to climb out in front of her. "Don't get angry, please, but do you need some help getting out?" she asked him gently.

"No, of course not," he said, wondering why she'd asked the question. And then it was clear. He hadn't moved, and she was worried. He was touched by her sensitivity. "I don't need any help, although I appreciate the thought. It's just that, well, I don't normally wear swim trunks. It won't bother me if it won't bother you," he concluded, his white, even teeth flashing in a grin.

Captivated by the way the smile changed the stern lines of his face, Karen felt the heat of a blush creep from her neck to her hairline. "I'll meet you on the patio," she said as she turned and walked out the door. She shut it behind her, but that didn't prevent sound from following her out of the heated room. She caught her breath in surprise, realizing that for the first time she'd heard the sound of David's laughter.

As she waited for him in the twilight haze of evening, a kind of peace descended over her. She closed her eyes, enjoying the soft wind on her face and the heady scent of late-blooming roses.

Some ten minutes later she heard the sliding door open and saw David standing there, a can of beer in his hand. "Can I interest you in one of these?"

"Thanks, I'd love one." The next thing she knew, he was back with a can of peanuts.

"I know you tend to be, er, hungry."

"How nice of you to remember." And she laughed. As she munched on the nuts he went back inside, this time returning with a can of beer for himself. Then he sat down in the chair across from her, his crutches on the floor beside him, his long legs extended in front of him. Every once in a while he massaged one leg or the other. She'd seen him make the gesture the night before. Was he tired after the swim? Or did that movement of his hand indicate pain?

As the silence between them stretched to awkward proportions, Karen found herself curiously reluctant to bring up anything that would destroy the fragile tranquillity of the moment. She cast about in her mind for something—anything—to say. What did she know about him, anyway? He was withdrawn. Moody. Angry. Couldn't those same words have been used to describe her own emotional tailspin in those first awful months after she'd lost Tim? Weren't some of the words still accurate? She had sought refuge in photography, David in his writing. He swam; so did she. "Do you work out in your pool every day?" she finally asked in desperation.

"Every day," he said with a nod. "It's part of the home physical therapy program the doctors came up with. They want me to conserve and develop what resources I've got, particularly upper-body strength."

From the way he'd looked even from a distance in the pool, the program must be working, Karen decided.

"Fortunately, I can do all that here," David was saying. "On my own. I've got what used to be the second bedroom outfitted as an exercise room. But my real love is the pool."

Mine, too, she added silently. "You're lucky that the pool came with the house," she said, not about to tell him how worried she'd been until she'd found him.

"I'm lucky there was a trust fund from my grandmother," he said almost to himself. "I'd never needed the money, so it just stayed in the bank, gathering interest. Then when I came back and decided to live on my own, I bought the house."

"But how could you go out and house hunt without seeing anyone?" she blurted. And when his mouth tightened grimly, she would have given anything to recall the words. To her surprise, the explosion she'd expected didn't come.

David took a sip of beer, then turned and looked out over the neatly kept grounds. "My best friend, Ken Friedman, is a lawyer. When I went overseas I gave him my power of attorney. When I came back I told him what I wanted and needed, and he arranged it. Once I moved in, I managed to get everything I needed delivered to the door. The telephone's a wonderful thing. Most of the things that need doing, like cooking, light cleaning, I manage by myself. I may be slow, but I get the job done. And when I need some kind of service like heavy cleaning or mowing the lawn, I contract out for it. The people who do that kind of thing know not to invade my privacy."

Too bad Karen Anderson didn't know the same thing, she was sure he must be thinking. "So did the pool come with the house, too?" she asked to cover her embarrassment.

"I had the garage converted and extended."

"It must be nice to be able to swim whenever you want."

He wondered at the touch of wistfulness in her tone. "Do you like to swim?"

"As often as I can. I try to go over to the Y every night after work. And sometimes I swim on my lunch hours and munch in the car between assignments. Swimming's one thing I can do and enjoy by myself. The Y's pool isn't fancy, but I don't need anything glitzy. I even keep a swimsuit in the car for emergencies, ever since one of my assignments called for me to do a photo essay on pool design."

"I guess all these trips back and forth to my place must have messed up your swim schedule."

"Like you said the other night, I'm getting paid to be here," she replied with a shrug.

He winced at that. "Ouch."

"Well—" she shrugged again "—I don't think I fit into the category of invited guest. Besides, I'll get my exercise back in sync soon enough." When Glen Larson finally relieved her of this assignment that wasn't an assignment.

"Coming out here must have played havoc with your social life, too."

"Social life?" she echoed.

"Men. I'm sure you date."

Why should he care about her social life or lack of it? "I don't recall asking what you do with your social life," she snapped.

"It doesn't exist."

"Ditto, as I've said before." The few casual dates she had hardly counted as a social life, which was just the way she wanted it.

His blue-eyed gaze raked her from head to toe and back again. "I find that hard to believe."

"I don't much care what you believe," she retorted, wishing she dared use the sweating beer can to cool the warmth of her cheeks. "The books are on the coffee table. Thanks for the beer," she said lightly as she got to her feet, sure that she'd worn out her dubious welcome.

That sounded like an exit line if there ever was one. But to his surprise and chagrin, David felt curiously reluctant to let Karen disappear into the sunset. "Stay and finish your beer," he suggested softly.

Barely managing to conceal her surprise, Karen sat down again, taking another sip. "Satisfy my curiosity. Why did you have me bring these books out here today, when just last night you apologized for all the wild-goose chases? What are you going to do when Larson finds out you're not working on the assignment—that all of my trips out here are costing the *Met* for gasoline and netting nothing? And since you don't deign to come into the building like the rest of us mere mortals, he'll yell at you on the phone or send you a note. I'm the one that will actually have to face him!"

"Karen," he cut in.

"Oh, what's the use?" she muttered in disgust, setting the half-finished beer on the flagstone surface as she prepared once more to leave. The steel-strong fingers of David's right hand fastened themselves gently but firmly around her left wrist.

"Karen, if you'll just listen! I needed those books. I didn't send you on a wild-goose chase."

"Sure." Her eyes focused in fascination on his long fingers linked around her flesh.

"Come inside with me."

"No, thanks. I can't stay. Tonight I'm actually going to treat myself to a real meal."

Removing his fingers from her wrist, he reached into his shirt pocket and handed her a folded piece of paper. "Why don't you have a look at this while I see how things are doing in the kitchen?" he suggested as he reached for the crutches and made his way to the sliding door.

"Why should I care how things are doing in the kitchen?" she muttered sullenly under her breath.

"Funny," he returned with a shrug, looking back at her through the doorway. "I thought you were the one who was always hungry."

"Very funny. Surely you must remember how it is?" she replied, fixing him with a pseudomalevolent stare. "When you're working on a story, or chasing all over town rounding up books, you're lucky if you get a dead candy bar to wolf down, let alone a meal. I'm even out of trail mix. The cupboard is bare."

"Read the paper, Karen," he urged from his position in the doorway. "It's only fair. After all, I read what you gave me last night. And I do broil a mean steak," he added.

"Steak?" she echoed.

"Read, Karen."

She watched him disappear into the house, then looked at the paper with the heading, "Prospective Interviews," which included names of people from all social and financial levels. Next to each name was a date for preliminary and follow-up question-and-answer sessions. Very comprehensive, she conceded. And then her heart gave a queer lurch as she read, "Ask Karen about photographic support needed." According to this, he was not only doing the assignment, he was even asking her opinion. Could this be yet another part of one of his elaborate snow jobs? If it was, why was he going to such lengths? And if it wasn't . . .

She trailed after him into the kitchen, mildly shocked to see him in an oversize apron. He was sitting on a stool and all around him she could see the makings of what looked to be a scrumptious dinner. To his left was a cutting board, on which reposed two thick steaks. And on his right were the makings for salad and dressing, as well as a pan of refrigerator rolls.

"How do you like your steak?"

"Medium rare."

"Fine. Maybe food will put you in a better mood."

"What do you care about my mood?" she challenged.

"Well, if we're going to be working together—"

"Like we have been?" she queried, her voice fairly dripping with sarcasm. She was surprised to see a trace of red appear on his cheekbones.

"Did you read the paper?" David asked steadily.

She was reminded of the night before, when she'd asked him virtually the same question about her note to him. "Yes, I read it. Very impressive." She didn't bother to conceal her skepticism.

David turned to face her, leaning against the kitchen counter for support. "It's for real. I did need the books to prepare for the interviews. I'm working on the first one starting today. Believe me yet?"

She was silent for a long moment, then couldn't resist another glance at the steaks. "I'm working on it. I'll let you know after I've tasted your steak."

He gave a shout of laughter. "Fair enough. We'll talk about it again after dinner, all right?"

"Fine," she agreed. Then, "Do you always eat like this?"

"Like what?"

"Oh, candles on the table. Wine." A gesture of her arm encompassed his preparations.

"Maybe I wanted to impress my new colleague."

"You didn't even know if I'd stay for dinner. A little sure of yourself, weren't you?" she suggested.

"Hopeful."

To that she made no reply, saying instead, "Can I help?"

"You can make the salad. The raw vegetables are all yours."

"Dressing, too?"

"Sure, go ahead. Live dangerously."

While concocting the salad and dressing, Karen had a chance to observe David at work. He seemed quite at home in the kitchen, as so many men were not, she noted as she munched thoughtfully on a carrot remnant. Of necessity, David's movements from one part of the room to the other were slow and steady. But once he came to a resting place such as a counter, or the edge of the oven, or the refrigerator, it was obvious he knew exactly what he was doing. And as she discovered later, he did broil a mean steak!

After dinner they had coffee in the living room, which was equipped with a wall unit complete with books and stereo components. The furniture was simple but eminently comfortable, Karen decided, settling back into the cream-colored armchair she'd used the night before.

"Karen?"

"Hmm?"

"Are you convinced yet about the assignment?"

"I'd like to believe you, but you just don't have a very good track record where I'm concerned."

"Well, I'm serious this time—never more so. No tricks on you or Larson." She shrugged as if she didn't care one way or the other, but he knew that was merely a cover-up. She'd told him from the first how important the assignment was to her. Now she looked resigned, displaying none of the feistiness he'd come to expect. Eyes narrowed, he got to his feet. "Don't go away," he ordered as he headed for his office. When he returned he sat down again, then leaned forward, extending his closed fist. "Maybe this will help convince you," he said. "Hold out your hand."

Intrigued, she did so, and watched him drop a piece of metal onto her open palm. It was a key, still warm from his touch. "What does this unlock?" she asked, her heart beating faster from his nearness.

"The doors to my house. You can come and go as you please. Nothing's off-limits."

Nothing except David Carter himself, she knew.

"And you won't have to stand outside and get wet if I don't hear the doorbell," he was saying. "I might be asleep, or in the pool like I was today. The methodology for this assignment was your idea. All I'm asking is for you to believe that I'm going to try damned hard to make it work for both of us. Do you believe me now?"

She looked down at the key in her hand, then back at David's face, which had never looked so open before. "Yes, I believe you," she whispered, slipping the key into her pocket.

Later that night she realized with a sense of awe what the key really meant: that he had at least a measure of trust in her, that he wasn't afraid she would come and go at the wrong times, that he was truly accepting her as a colleague. She held the key tightly in her hand and wondered if she would ever be accepted as anything else. A friend, perhaps? Only time would tell.

6

DAVID WAS TRUE to his word. There were no more wild-goose chases, no more retakes for no reason. He could really be quite considerate when he wanted to. He showed a real interest in the photographs she was taking for the assignment. Perversely, however, she saw considerably less of him as the assignment actually started rolling and he began interviewing in earnest.

He had his list of people to talk to. An entire interview might take two or perhaps three telephone sessions, he'd warned Karen. And then there was the preliminary and follow-up research she coordinated with him, searching the *Met* library's files when necessary. Whenever the phone rang in her apartment, she was more than likely to hear David's baritone on the other end of the line, apprising her of his progress.

"Have a nice weekend," he told her when he spoke to her on the phone at the end of their second full week of really working together. "I'll see you on Monday." He would rather have seen her all weekend. But Karen was very dangerous to his emotional equilibrium. Just being in the same room with her raised his pulse rate and body temperature. Sometimes he even had trouble breathing.

He looked over at the pile of notes that represented his first attempt at a telephone interview for this assignment. Maybe working on his article on Mrs. Adrian Wyatt would block thoughts of Karen

Anderson. He paid no attention to the snide voice that taunted, *You've got to be kidding! Bet you can't do it!*

"Bet you I can," he muttered to himself. He had to.

Karen spent Friday evening in her darkroom, developing pictures of the Wyatt mansion, which she'd visited earlier in the week. Since Mrs. Wyatt was the subject of David's first interview, Karen wanted to give him her best effort. It was nearly midnight when she closed up shop, tired but satisfied. She felt so good about the results that she couldn't resist calling him and telling him about it first thing Saturday morning. "How's the Wyatt piece coming?" she asked him.

"Let's talk about something else," he said with a groan.

"Never mind. I have some really good shots of the interior and exterior of the grounds and, of course, of the lady herself. If you want to see them, I can bring them over this morning."

He would have liked nothing better. He was more than ready to admit, at least to himself, that he enjoyed her company. "That's not fair to you. It messes up your weekend."

And lets you have more solitary time to yourself, she added silently. How could she tell him that weekends meant less than nothing to her, that she had no one special to spend them with, unless she drove down to visit her parents? "So Saturday will start a little later."

"I took it for granted you'd be busy. I seem to recall you weren't at all anxious to work on Saturdays several weeks ago."

"I seem to recall that the last time I worked for you on a Saturday, it was because of one of your patented make-work projects," she reminded him tartly.

"Touché." He laughed. "Maybe seeing the photographs would help, after all, if you don't mind the trip out here. At this point the piece isn't hanging together any too well. Maybe what you have will help me get my thinking on track."

"I don't mind," she assured him.

He listened for the sound of her car, and, nearly an hour later, was at the front door before she had time to ring the bell. He laughed heartily at her sweatshirt, which bore the legend, Photographers Give You the Eye. The shirt was worn over jeans that were just tight enough to mold the sweetly rounded outline of her derriere and her slender legs. He swallowed hard, barely able to keep from saying, *You sure were worth waiting for.* "Thanks a lot for coming," he said aloud, his voice noticeably rougher than usual. "I'm sorry to have broken up your day." *And you've certainly made mine*, he added to himself.

"No problem," she assured him with a grin, delighted by the laughter her sweatshirt had prompted. That was why she'd worn it. David needed to laugh more, she'd long since decided. "I didn't have anything special planned, just some lap time at the pool. Saturday mornings are good for me, because in the afternoons there are dozens of screaming elementary-school kids pretending to be in the Olympics!"

"That doesn't sound conducive to lap swimming."

"That's an understatement."

He cleared his throat with difficulty. "Didn't you once tell me that you always have a suit with you?" When she nodded, he said rather diffidently, "You can do your laps here. Alone. Nobody will bother you." So much for maintaining distance, he acknowledged wryly, cursing his own weakness.

She struggled to keep her mouth from dropping open in sheer surprise. "Here?" she squeaked.

"I had thought I was speaking in plain English. The David Carter Country Club is open for business. You are cordially invited to this exclusive establishment—"

Cordial my foot! "All right, already. I get the message." She laughed again, startled by his unaccustomed flash of humor.

"And lunch is on me. Don't worry about the food," he added gruffly. "If you can spare me the time, the least I can do is feed you. I guess I'd better get used to it."

What a graceful invitation that was, she noted with chagrin. "Thanks a lot. I'll get my suit. Will you be swimming, too?" she asked almost as an afterthought, recalling that he'd said she would be swimming alone.

"Why? Would it bother you to be in the pool with me?" he rasped.

Wonderful. She'd done it again, rubbed him the wrong way, trod on what she knew were sensitive areas. "No, of course not," she replied hurriedly, afraid her thoughtless words had already made him regret his impulsive invitation.

"But I thought you usually liked to swim alone, Karen."

"I just meant that it's an exercise I can do without a partner, unlike tennis or racketball. Do you think the Y lets me have the pool to myself? Well, think again! In fact, I think I might be better off going to swim there, after all."

"No," he replied without hesitation, his blue eyes glaring at her.

She glared right back at him. "Give me a good reason why not. After all, it's pretty clear that if I use the pool, you won't. So just look the photographs over at your leisure."

"Wait."

There was a taut, strained look on his face, one that she would have given anything to erase. Permanently.

"There are other scars," he said.

"I can be remarkably nearsighted," she assured him softly.

He took a deep breath, then raised his head, sending her a half smile. "Does that mean you expect me to wear trunks?" he asked lightly.

Her heart caught at the twinkle that suddenly appeared in his deep blue eyes. "I'm not that nearsighted!"

"I was afraid of that," he said with a wry grin. "Go get your suit."

"It won't take me long. And by the way, when I asked if you'd be swimming, too, I was just concerned about invading your privacy."

To her surprise, he threw back his head and laughed, the sound continuous and carefree, as she had never heard it before. "What did I say?" she asked, staring at him in amazement.

He coughed several times before he was finally able to speak. "Karen, you've done nothing but invade my privacy ever since I've met you. Why should the pool be off-limits?" When she made no reply, he queried, "Cat got your tongue, lady?"

"Just trying to figure out something suitable. And failing. I'll meet you in the pool," she said, hurrying back to her car.

Despite her best efforts, she could feel herself blushing as she went to retrieve her carryall. In the bathroom, she slipped into the sapphire-blue maillot and then into the matching long-sleeved terry jacket that ended just at the tops of her slender thighs. She couldn't help wondering what David would think when he saw her. The suit was conservative by resort standards, cut in a modest V that just revealed the tops of her breasts, but low in the back and high on the sides. She pinned her hair and gathered it into an elasticized band so that it wouldn't get in her way.

While David waited for Karen to join him, he immersed himself in the water, doing a series of warm-up laps, continually casting an eye toward the door she would soon walk through, admitting to himself that he couldn't wait until she was in the pool with him.

When Karen got to the door of the converted garage, she realized anew that this wasn't just another swimming pool she was going to. It was David's pool, and he would be in it with her. As she went inside the heated room, she paused to watch him swim, his powerful arms and muscular body working in perfect harmony as he propelled himself through the water with rhythmic strokes.

As she stood in the doorway, she knew he'd seen her, for he stopped in midlap, waved and began swimming to the side of the pool, anchoring himself at the edge. Waiting for her.

"Come on in and shut the door," he called good-naturedly. "We don't want to heat up the living room, now do we?"

"No, of course not." She took a deep breath, feeling self-conscious under his scrutiny.

"Do you usually swim in a robe?" he asked.

She could feel her face grow warm. "Of course not," she answered, shrugging out of the cover-up and laying it on the bench beside his robe, the one she'd worn the night of the rainstorm.

He watched her doff the cover-up—and felt his heart begin to pound. She was exquisite. The sapphire blue of the French-cut suit contrasted with the creamy ivory of her skin. His eyes traveled the length of her body, from the crown of her head, with her hair gathered back into a pony tail, to her slender waist, to her long, slim legs. "Come on in," he invited, struggling to keep his voice even. "The water's fine."

She smiled at the cliché, then descended the four steps into the pool, which was perhaps four-and-a-half feet deep. Breast high for her. The water was pleasantly, seductively warm. With very little effort, she could lose herself in that warmth. David was positioned half a length away from her.

He stayed where he was, swallowing hard as he saw how the buoyancy of the water supported Karen's breasts. Even from his position perhaps fifteen feet away, he could see the outlines of her thrusting nipples against the tautness of the fabric. He felt a painful tightening in his loins as it was graphically brought home to him what effect a nearly naked woman could have on him after all that time. And not just any woman. Karen Anderson. He very nearly lost his grip on the side of the pool. He knew he would have to get away from her before they were both embarrassed. What he really needed was a cold shower, not a warm swimming pool!

"How many laps do you usually do?" he asked, striving for normalcy.

"Fifty, for starters."

"The pool's only half a regulation lap long," he reminded.

"Then I guess I'll have to multiply by two," she said with a laugh, then swam the length of the pool to where he waited so that they'd be swimming in the same direction and not running into each other.

She had meant to begin swimming right away, but the sight of David stopped her. Oh, not the scars on his face, which she hardly noticed, or the ones on his legs, which she could see through the water. Souvenirs from past surgeries. No, it was his superbly conditioned body that captivated her. She could see the results of his efforts to develop upper-body strength. He was muscular but not muscle-bound. The broad chest with its wet pelt of hair led to a lean waist. She swallowed as her gaze was drawn farther down to where his body was bisected by the tight, black briefs. And though his legs might not have been strong enough for him to walk unaided, they were well-shaped, with no signs of atrophy. Not that it would have mattered to her. "I—I think we should start swimming," she suggested hurriedly, admitting to herself for the first time that she would much rather stare at her host than swim in his pool!

"Sure," he agreed instantly.

With a nod, she was off, heading for the opposite side of the pool, mentally counting laps. David was in the far lane, she in the near one. She had almost forgotten his presence when she felt a jolt that briefly knocked her off balance. But then, as suddenly as it happened, a pair of immensely strong hands grasped her upper arms, guiding her toward the surface.

"What!" she gasped, coughing from the effects of swallowed water.

"I'm sorry," he said, still holding on to her. "I'm not used to swimming with anyone. I didn't mean to get into your lane."

"It's—okay. I—I thought for a minute you were playing water games."

David stared at the woman he held at arm's length. "Not likely. Are you all right?" He steadied her with one hand while using the other to push wet hair back from his forehead.

"Fine. I'm fine," she answered, mesmerized by the sight of the jagged scar on his left temple. She hadn't seen the extent of it before; it was usually covered by the fullness of his hair. She shivered, realizing how very close he'd come to death, amazed at her own depth of feeling. She had been so long in an emotional deep freeze but now she could almost feel his pain.

"Have you seen enough?" David snapped, blue fire flashing from his eyes as he registered Karen's scrutiny.

"I didn't mean to stare," she said defensively. And then, before she could stop herself, she reached up to trace the length of the scar with her fingers.

He tensed but managed not to flinch as he saw her hand come toward his face. And it was soon over, her touch so light that he half wondered if he'd imagined it. Her next words startled him.

"Do you want to do some more laps?" she asked, hoping she hadn't ruined the day.

He took a deep breath, letting it out slowly. He'd already worked out on the equipment before Karen had come. "I think I'll just hang around the side and watch."

"I won't be long," she assured him.

"Take your time."

In a moment she was back in her lane, swimming flat out.

At first he thought she was trying to prove her superiority. Even though working on the equipment and swimming strengthened him, he knew he would never have the form and style she had. He looked at her. She was swimming with a kind of desperation. Finally he couldn't stand it any longer. He waited until she was approaching his end of the pool before he moved over to her lane to meet her.

Unawares, she came up against a hard masculine chest and backed off, afraid she'd hurt him, almost losing her balance in her efforts. Strong hands biting into her upper arms prevented that, steadying her. "What's wrong?" she panted, trying to get her breath.

He brushed long strands of hair back from her face. "I was going to ask you that."

She looked at him blankly. "I don't understand."

"You swim as if you're in training, as if you were trying for a medal."

"I always swim like that. I—just want to keep in shape."

He surveyed her slender form from head to toe and back, his gaze returning to her parted lips, heaving breasts and the spiky wetness of her lashes. He felt his heart shift into high gear at her nearness. "I think we can safely say you're certainly accomplishing that goal."

"I wouldn't tell *you* what to do," she replied, full lips pouting slightly.

He laughed. "Since when?"

Despite the easy good humor in his expression, she knew she'd been rude. "I'm sorry. I didn't mean to snap. I'm really not out to shatter any world records, honestly. You swim well," she added, hoping to change the subject.

So much for finding out why she was trying to be a female Mark Spitz. "Thanks. How about some lunch?

I've got the makings for cold-cut subs. You can have onions or not. What do you say?"

Glad that the awkward moment had passed, she said yes to the subs and no to the onions. "That's definitely an offer I can't refuse. It won't take me long to change into dry clothes and wring out my hair."

"No hurry. I'll get things set up."

"WHAT'S HAPPENING at the *Met*?" he asked her perhaps forty-five minutes later, once they'd finished building their subs and had settled down to eat them.

"Well, the old presses are gone; they're going to use the space for offices. The photography department equipment needs to be replaced before there's a major breakdown. And of course, there's gossip. But you might not want to hear it...."

"Talk, lady."

Glad to see that she'd piqued his interest, she leaned forward conspiratorially, telling him that X had gone out to the West Coast to head a bureau. Another bureau chief had been unhappy, come back to the paper and had been made the Metro editor. Y had gotten married to Z, but one wrote for the morning edition, the other for the evening paper. "No joint bylines there," he quipped.

W had just left for a three-year tour of Central America, Karen continued. That was a mistake, she knew right away, as the lively look of interest on David's face changed to a scowl. Trying to recoup, she told him how C had just gone on maternity leave with her husband. And finished up by saying that the new baseball writer was a woman.

He laughed. "That's a switch."

"Chauvinist!" she returned in kind, relieved at his lightened mood.

AS DAVID COURTED SLEEP later that night, he had recurring visions of Karen Anderson: either dressed as an urchin, soaking wet, enveloped in his robe or as she'd looked today, in a skintight swimsuit. What would she be like naked, he wondered, her breasts freed from the confines of the sapphire-blue covering. Closing his eyes, he could imagine her swimming laps, clothed only in warm water, the wet length of her hair and the touch of his hands.

Several cold showers separated Saturday night from Sunday morning.

MONDAY MORNING DAWNED bright and clear. Karen could hardly wait to get back to David's house for the planning session he'd mentioned just before she'd left on Saturday afternoon. The weekend should have given him time to review all the photographs she'd taken, as well as allowing him time to integrate his notes into a coherent article.

When David opened the door for her, the first thing he said was, "I should have called and told you not to come."

"Good morning to you, too!"

"Oh, hell, I'm not angry at you, Karen. I just didn't get much of anything accomplished. Come on in," he said half-heartedly.

"Still working on the Wyatt piece?"

"Still," he confirmed, heading back to his office.

She followed, stopping at the doorway as she gazed at the sea of crumpled paper that surrounded his chair. "It's not coming, I take it?"

"Let's put it this way. I've had easier times coming to the words, The End."

"Writer's block?"

"Something like that," he replied, raking a hand through his already disordered hair.

"I know the feeling."

"You write?" he asked without looking up at her.

Only notes to recalcitrant journalists, she felt like saying, recalling only too well the note that had accompanied her photograph of him. "No, I wouldn't say that I write. But sometimes I mean to take a picture, and something isn't right. It just isn't working. It could be mood, or lighting or composition. For whatever reason, it won't hang together, no matter what I do. Want a second opinion?" Karen asked gingerly, not knowing how he'd react to her suggestion.

For a moment he was utterly still. "You wouldn't mind?"

"Not if I could be of some help," she replied diffidently.

"All right. You're on."

Minutes later Karen had scanned and then closely read the entire article. He was right; there was something wrong with it. It had no vitality; it certainly couldn't compare with the pieces he'd written before his injury. But she couldn't very well tell him that. He didn't know she'd read his files.

"Well?" he demanded, his voice intruding on her thoughts.

"It's a little flat, I think. But of course I'm no writer," she hastened to remind him.

"No." He sighed, reclaiming the piece and setting it aside. "But you *are* a reader. And I agree with you."

"Are you open to suggestions?"

"Shoot."

"I think you should interview Mrs. Wyatt in person."

He leaned back in his chair, fixing her with a baleful glare. "No."

"You haven't even considered it."

"There's nothing to consider."

"It was just an idea," she put in lamely.

"A damned lousy one. I'd probably scare her to death."

Karen was wise enough not to try to disagree with him. He obviously wasn't in the mood. "How about another suggestion, then?"

"Your track record is less than impressive," he commented dryly. "But I know you won't let that stop you."

"Thanks for the vote of confidence. Oh, well, here goes. Why don't you back off, get away from it for a while?"

"You mean work on another piece?"

"No, I mean get out of your house and away from here."

"What do you suggest, Madame Travel Agent?" he demanded in a voice laden with sarcasm. "Should I take a cruise, or run through the hills, a walk in the woods, a bicycle tramp? You name it, social director!"

She cringed at the roughness of his words "That isn't what I meant. You could go out—"

"On a date? Got anybody in mind? Never mind. Forget it."

Mentally she counted to ten, then added another ten for good measure. Obtuse. The man was obtuse. "David, my car's got a full tank of gas. We could go for a drive. A picnic, even."

"It's October."

"It's eighty degrees. Indian summer."

"All right. We'll have a picnic. Anything to keep you happy. Front yard or back yard? It was your idea, so you choose."

"I—I was thinking of a different location, actually. There's a park near my parents' house in Annapolis."

"No! Besides, even if I don't work on the Wyatt piece, I've got a column to write."

"When's it due?"

"Yesterday. I write every day, you know that."

"Pen and paper are pretty portable, aren't they?"

"I don't know what you're getting at."

"You could take your notes with you."

"No! I like it where I am. It works for me this way. I'm not having everybody stare at me. And if you don't like it, you've got a home. Don't let me keep you from it," he concluded abruptly.

"That's always your answer, isn't it? 'Take a powder. Go away. Don't bother me. Leave me alone.' Well, fine. I think maybe I will." With that she turned on her heel and headed for the door.

"What is it with you anyway, lady? Aren't you ever satisfied? I—I've let you into my life, for heaven's sake!"

"Yes, but you haven't let life into you," she said quietly as she walked briskly to her car.

"And you haven't walked in my shoes!" he shouted after her. *She's bluffing,* he told himself. Then he heard the unmistakable sound of her car. He'd called her bluff. And lost. He went to the window and watched her drive away.

"What a waste of a beautiful day," Karen muttered to herself disgustedly. "He wants to rot, let him rot. Why should I care? Drat the man!" But before she'd driven more than a mile, her temper began to cool.

What could I have been thinking of, she asked herself. *What did I think I could gain by trying to pressure him into doing something he obviously hates? Why couldn't I have left well enough alone?* And then she recalled his parting words: "You haven't walked in my shoes."

He was right, Karen acknowledged as she turned around at the first cross street she could and drove back to David's house. She didn't bother to ring his doorbell. For the first time she pulled out the key he'd given her several weeks before.

He was in the pool, swimming flat out, as she herself did so often. She quickly closed the door behind her, relieved that he didn't notice as she slipped in and out of the room. And that he didn't notice as she picked up the crutches leaning against the bench.

In all this time, she'd never touched them. But they were so much an extension of David that they didn't feel strange to her at all. They were surprisingly lightweight, because they were made mostly of aluminum. She took them into the living room, slipping one slender forearm into the split at the front of each cuff, then wrapped her hands around the ridged horizontal plastic grips. And then she tried to do as she had seen David do so often: walk.

Of course, the cuffs were too large for her; they were positioned to fit David's massive forearms. And the poles themselves were the wrong height. Naturally, as soon as she tried to walk, her feet got tangled in the poles, so she had to start the process all over again. By that time, her palms were sweaty on the plastic grips and the cuffs had slid well past her forearms, threatening to cut into her elbows. She began again, taking small, lurching steps, her goal being a walk around the perimeter of the living room. She cleared her mind, forcing herself to think of nothing but establishing a rhythm. She lost track of time, even of place, as she concentrated. And then one of the poles caught in the nap of the rug, and she went down on the floor with a thud.

DAVID SWAM to the side of the pool. The vigorous exercise hadn't helped him come up with a new angle on the article, or on the lady whose temper had such a short fuse. Of course, he wasn't exactly a master of calm himself, he admitted wryly as he planted his palms on the side of the pool and levered himself out.

At first he thought he was seeing things. The towels and the terry robe were on the bench. But the crutches were gone. He looked on the floor to see if they'd fallen. Nothing.

He reached for a towel and dried himself. After he'd managed to seat himself on the bench, he put on the robe, belting it tightly. Then, taking a deep breath, he made his way from the bench to the door and down the hallway. His progress was slow, since his ability to function without the crutches was limited at best. As he neared the living room he heard the familiar sound of the crutches at work—the creak of metal against metal, the uneven rhythm of shifting feet. And then there were other sounds—a crash, followed by a yelp of pain.

David gritted his teeth as he tried to quicken his pace, hanging on to the wall or an occasional piece of furniture for support. When he got to the living room, he found his crutches. They were attached to Karen's arms. His eyes widening in disbelief, he fought not to lose his temper with her again. Taking a deep breath, he said matter-of-factly, "Tell me this isn't some kind of sick joke."

Karen half turned, her mouth dropping open in shock as she looked up at the man towering over her. "David! How did you manage?" Her concern for him eclipsed her apprehension at the anger he was probably feeling.

"Slowly and carefully," he commented with a grim smile as he sank down gratefully onto the sofa. "Which is more than I can say for you. Are you all right?"

She nodded as she slid her arms out of the cuffs, then gingerly placed the crutches within easy reach of his hands. Bending her head, she turned away from him. "You said I hadn't walked in your shoes," she said softly.

"Is that why—" At her nod, he reached down for her hand. "Did you hurt yourself?"

She shook her head as she leaned against the edge of the sofa. "Just my pride. It looks so easy when you do it."

"Practice makes perfect." He saw her wince. "I wasn't being sarcastic, believe me. I spent a lot of time in physical therapy, even before the casts were off and the stitches out. Even before I was out of the wheelchair, they had me on a slant board, then working with weights, and then the parallel bars. And that all continued once I was put on crutches. And Karen, the first thing those medical drill instructors taught us was how to fall."

"Did you fall?"

"A lot." He laughed. "As you said: just my pride. There was always someone there to make sure I didn't really hurt myself, though. Come on, let me help you up," he urged, extending his hands to her.

Without hesitation she put her hands in his, marveling at his controlled strength as he bent forward to help her to the sofa beside him without seeming to exert himself at all. She tugged at her hands to free them, but he held on, turning her hands over. As he'd expected, her palms were reddened slightly and still held the impression of the hard plastic hand grips. He stroked his thumbs lightly across the palms. "If you'd used these crutches for any length of time, these reddened areas would have become blistered."

"You don't have blisters."

He released her hands to rest his own hands in her lap, palms up.

She was struck by the innocence of the gesture. Almost without volition, she touched him as he'd touched her, her fingers finding ridged hardness. Unbelievably, his flesh seemed to tremble at her touch. She looked up quickly, uncertain of his reaction—and lost herself in the arrestingly soft look in his blue eyes.

"My blisters were replaced by calluses a long time ago." Then a thought occurred to him. "What would you have done if I'd been using the crutches, Karen? Asked for a tryout?"

Encouraged by the suggestion of a smile on his lips, she answered honestly, "I probably would have stopped at the first pharmacy or medical equipment place and rented a pair of them for a day or so."

"Why doesn't that surprise me?" He shook his head ruefully. "I'm sorry I lashed out at you before. I—"

She laid a silencing finger across his lips. "So am I. I had no right to say what I did, or to leave in a huff."

"You were right."

"To leave?"

"No." He sighed. "You were right in suggesting that I get out of here. I'm so damned insulated, although," he added candidly, "I don't think I realized just how much until you showed up. Anyway, if you're still game for a picnic—"

"You bet!" she answered with a grin.

"All right. Give me a chance to get dry and dressed, and we'll figure out a place."

"I'll tell you what, you do that while I go out and rustle up a bucket of fried chicken."

"My treat."

She rose stiffly from the sofa. "It was my idea," she countered. "Besides, you're always feeding me."

"That's true enough."

"Thanks a lot!"

"Hey, I'm just agreeing with you. Okay, it's your treat."

7

BY THE TIME she returned forty-five minutes later, David was waiting outside for her. He was wearing jeans and a fisherman-knit sweater. Karen was also wearing jeans, along with a cotton-knit shirt and the ever-present khaki jacket with its many pockets. And, of course, her cameras were in the car. Even though she wouldn't be working, she never went anywhere without them. She only hoped David's chosen picnic spot had some interesting scenery.

"Need any help?" she called casually through the car window. She didn't want to offend him by offering assistance where none was wanted or needed.

"No, I don't think so, but if I do, you'll be the first to know," he said as he made his way to the passenger side and opened the door. He moved carefully until the backs of his legs were touching the edge of the seat. Then he planted the tips of the crutches firmly in the turf, balanced himself and eased into a sitting position. Once he'd slid his forearms from the cuffs, he twisted around to stow the crutches in the back of the car. After he'd shifted his legs into the car, he sighed heavily and said, "Ready anytime you are."

"Aren't you glad you're getting out, David? Admit it!"

"Well, I hate to admit it, but I guess I am." He laughed sheepishly.

"So how about a face-to-face interview? If one of my ideas is a winner . . ."

"Don't be obnoxious, Karen."

"You mean I shouldn't press my luck?"

"Something like that."

"I thought it was worth a try."

"Thought I was 'easy'?"

They both laughed.

"You could start with someone you've interviewed in the past. It wouldn't be like blazing new territory; it would be kind of like a follow-up."

"No! And don't get any bright ideas about bringing anyone to my house. I won't be home to them, or you. Got it?"

"In one," she muttered.

"Now, if you're ready to go on this picnic . . ."

She exchanged glances with him and started the engine. "Okay. This is your party. The gas tank is full. Where to?"

"About seventy miles due southwest of here."

"Where are we going?"

"Sugar Loaf Mountain." His words seemed to drop into a well of silence. "Do you know where it is?"

"I'll find it," she said grimly.

"You sound less than enthusiastic."

If he only knew, she thought, agonized, swallowing hard. And if he did, would he care? "Oh, I was just hoping that you might like to picnic at some place like the reservoir, or maybe the lake in Columbia."

"Terrific. Lots of cute little ducks and swans—and little kids who'll get scared to death if they see me."

"Forget I mentioned the reservoir and the lake." She sighed. "What's at Sugar Loaf Mountain?" she asked after several more miles.

"You'll love it," he insisted. "It's a very high, grassy overlook, with a great view of the Blue Ridge Mountains. Years ago the land was given to the state for use as a public park. We're really fortunate to have all that beauty."

"Oh, yes. Very fortunate," Karen echoed bleakly, wondering how she was going to cope. "What does Sugar Loaf mean to you?"

"It's just about my favorite place in Maryland. I always used to go up there when I wanted to just be by myself, tramp around, think things through."

"You could still come up here if you had a car."

"Right. And pigs can fly!"

"Cars can be adapted for hand use, David. Surely you know that."

"Of course I know that! I'm just not ready for it." Privately he doubted if he'd ever be ready for it. In an effort to steer the conversation back to a more comfortable subject, he asked, "Did you bring your cameras?"

"Of course." She was glad that his formidable temper had evidently cooled. "My fingers start to itch if my cameras aren't close by."

Much too soon for Karen's liking, they arrived at their destination. She directed the car up a narrow trail, trying not to think of the steepness of the grade. Her concentration was broken when David told her to park on a narrow, graveled overlook. He was out of the car almost as soon as she cut the engine. She didn't move. Her fingers were practically fused to the steering wheel.

When she was able to risk a glance out her window, she could only look away quickly, muttering, "How am I going to go through with this?" How was she going to find the courage to get out of the car, let alone stick around for a picnic! She brushed sweating palms against the sides of her jeans and carefully opened the door. Then, she went to the trunk, taking out the blanket he had provided as a ground cover. Afterwards, her mouth grew parched with fear as she watched David make his way slowly toward the edge of the cliff. But her fear for him faded as she realized he was more sure-footed on his crutches than she was on two perfectly good legs.

"This is great! What are you waiting for?" he called, a previously unheard, almost playful tone in his voice. "You've got to come and look at all this. There isn't even any haze. You can almost see the Washington Monument!"

She winced at his enthusiasm. He was seated about four feet from the edge of the drop, his back propped against a massive rock. Shuddering, Karen swallowed with difficulty. "Coming." She leaned against the car, biting down hard on her lower lip. Then she walked in slow motion to David's rock. With awful clarity, she saw that he was actually bending forward. The blanket she was carrying dropped from her nerveless fingers.

Hearing her footsteps behind him, David turned. "You can fix the blanket later. The view won't wait."

It could wait forever, she wanted to say as she allowed herself to be drawn to where he was sitting, his crutches within easy reach.

"There's plenty of room," he encouraged, smiling up at her briefly before turning his head once more to the scene in the distance.

He actually expected her to get even closer, she realized with a sinking feeling. She went as far as she dared. It was as if she were welded to the ageless rock, her feet rooted to the ground, her upper body weightless. And even though she wasn't looking, she knew the edge of the world was there—the entrance to some giant abyss that yawned before her.

She was cold; the khaki jacket offered scant protection against the sudden chill that seemed to come from within her, from her very bones. The bright sunlight blurred and wavered, turning everything a dull gray. And then there was only black as she was caught in a sickening vortex, falling, always falling, having no choice but to let gravity pull her to the ground.

David heard a rustle, turned in time to see Karen sway, then watched with a sense of shock as her eyes closed and she started to fall forward. With a massive effort, he launched himself toward her, managing to catch her upper arms in an iron grip before she could hit the rocky ground.

"Karen, for God's sake, what's wrong?" There was no answer. She hung limply in his arms, her head forward, practically resting on his chest. He pulled her into his lap, holding her close as he cradled her slight body against his own. The pulse in her wrist was rapid. He bent his head, touching his lips to her forehead. Her skin was cold and clammy.

Holding her carefully within the shelter of one arm, he reached back with the other hand for the blanket she'd dropped. He pulled it around her as best he could, then wrapped both his arms around her, rocking her gently. He held her against his heart, fiercely protective of the woman who had somehow managed to work her way past the defenses he'd erected so long ago. Pressing her head into the hollow of his shoulder, he gently stroked her hair, wondering what on earth was wrong. He felt a searing anger at himself for the weakness that rendered him helpless to do more than hold her in his arms.

For so long he had felt trapped by his own condition, unaware, even uncaring of the needs of others. What folly, to be trapped with all the comforts of home and able to get all he physically wanted or needed just by lifting the telephone. Now, in a critical situation, he wondered how he'd cope. Why had he ever suggested such an out-of-the-way place? From cowardice, of course, came the answer from deep within. He'd craved the isolation, the sure knowledge that he need see no one. And that he needed no one. Now he was alone, at the mercy of the elements, Karen helpless in his arms. He felt truly alone. It was ironic. Now he would have given anything for the sight of another human being. He couldn't make it down the mountain by himself. And even if he could, he would never leave Karen behind. What if she were seriously ill? What if . . .

His agonized thoughts were interrupted by a faint moan. Quickly he put his fingers to the side of her throat. Her skin was still cold, but her pulse beat more strongly, thank God. Encouraged by the faint sound, he rubbed her arms through the rough wool of the blanket.

She was trembling with cold and from the aftermath of shock. "I have to get you warmed up," he whispered as she sighed audibly. Freeing one hand, he gathered her blanket-wrapped form once more into his arms. Her need for him was a potent aphrodisiac, her nearness a unique kind of sensual torture. He was trying to shield her from the cold, while he fought to control his body's reaction, the burning heat that radiated through him with every beat of his heart. In her unconscious state, she seemed to cling to him, her boneless slenderness molding to him almost as if she were a part of him. And he— "God help me," David groaned, clasping her closer still. "I feel as if I'm a part of her...."

KAREN WAS WRAPPED in a black cocoon from which there was no escape. She felt the pull of light against darkness. She willed it to continue as strong, gentle hands touched her body. She wasn't really hearing words but responding to the caring voice that cut through the layers of darkness. Like an animal seeking warmth in the dead of winter, she burrowed into the hard, masculine warmth of an embrace that seemed to represent safety, security and so much more.

One hand cupped the back of her head, pressing her cheek gently against the cabled wool of his sweater. His other hand made delicate forays up and down her slender back. Through half-closed eyes she was vaguely aware of the dark, curly hair at the base of his throat and wondered if it felt as soft as it looked. His heart beat strongly, rhythmically against her cheek, almost lulling her into a truly restful sleep.

Slowly the nightmare receded, the thick layers of black fading first to gray, then to milky opaqueness. Memory and experience interlocked, transmuting nightmare into the golden brightness of a dream, a wonderful dream. Slowly the hand returned, this time stroking her cheek. Concentrating all her strength, she managed to grasp that masculine hand and press her lips to its palm.

Electrified by her extraordinary gesture, he curled his fingers into his palm, as if to preserve the feel of her lips against his callused flesh. He saw her eyelids flutter, saw her throat move as she swallowed. And then he watched, unbearably moved, as she rested her head trustingly against the support of his arm.

He traced the delicate hollow of her cheek, felt his heart contract as her breast rose and fell in a deep sigh. "Karen," he murmured, unable to resist the inexorable pull of gravity that drew him to the softness of her mouth. His kiss was weightless, his lips barely brushing hers.

The touch of his mouth was incendiary, warming her from the inside out, melting forever the layers of ice that had encased her heart for too long. Forgetting everything, even where she was, she arched toward him, desperately needing to return the kiss of life he'd given her. "My love," she breathed.

"I'm not your love," he said bluntly, the words torn from him.

Karen's eyes snapped open at the harshness of the voice that eclipsed the dream. She looked up into the face of the man hovering over her and felt the living nightmare return. "Oh, God," she moaned, shutting her eyes tightly, her head turning from side to side, tears sliding from under her closed lids.

David flinched as if struck, finally realizing the bitter truth. Her response to him was no different than anyone else's; she'd simply managed to conceal it until now. After all, he was her stake in the future. That damned assignment! What a fool he'd been to believe anything else. "You don't have to shut your eyes," he muttered, wishing he didn't have to endure the almost physical pain of continuing to hold her in his arms. Then, with a semblance of self-control, he asked, "Why didn't you tell me you were ill? We didn't have to come here."

"Or anywhere else, for that matter," she cut in shakily, mentally cursing the weakness that was evident even in her voice. "I'm not sick."

"You could have fooled me! Why did you faint? And don't bother to tell me you didn't. I was here, and you were out like a light!"

"There's nothing wrong with me," she insisted, wishing he would let it go and simply let her lie there until she was strong enough to move under her own power.

Nothing was wrong with her, he echoed silently. Nothing except a face that was paper white, tear streaked. He had helped make it that way, after all. And there was no point in thinking about the exquisitely tender, even welcoming expression on her face when she'd first opened her eyes. It hadn't been for him; that was clear enough. "Tell me why you fainted."

She swallowed hard. "Tim—my husband." She tried to look anywhere but at David, but found that she couldn't. The view made her dizziness return. "He loved climbing."

David had a sinking feeling he knew what was coming next.

"He used to teach mountain climbing at one of the community colleges out here. He'd taken a group of kids out one weekend. Two years ago. To the Catoctin Mountains."

Her voice was brittle, like dry leaves drifting to earth on autumn air. "Karen, you don't have to go on."

She ignored him, willing herself to keep on saying the words that she knew had caused—would continue to cause—infinite pain, perhaps because she knew David, too, had suffered deep hurt and would understand her own. "One of those kids that day was determined to be a show-off. Tim had to try and get him off a ledge. There was—an accident."

"You were there." It was a statement, not a question.

"I thought he would never stop f-falling."

Impulsively David reached out, grasping Karen's ice-cold hands.

She held herself stiffly, carefully, trying to keep her body from shaking, trying to concentrate on not breaking down completely and making a fool of herself. For a moment she yielded to weakness—and temptation—and let her fingers rest in the warm strength of his. "I'm fine now. Really." Then she made the mistake of looking up into his face.

But I'm not, he said to himself. "I know this isn't what you want."

She stiffened, then backed away from him until her head was just touching the support of his arm. His features were stiff, as if he were in pain. And his blue eyes were flat, cold stones. Dead. "What are you talking about?"

"When you came to a while ago, you looked up and saw my face."

Vaguely she remembered being caught between the mist of dreams and the wonder of growing passion. But her memory of those moments was too hazy to separate one from the other. "What happened?"

He could only shake his head.

"David." When he didn't respond, she lifted one hand and laid it gently against the side of his jaw, feeling him flinch as she touched the furrow of his scar. "Did I hurt you? Strike you?" Maybe her own vision of reality, of the kiss they'd shared, was different from his. "I—I don't remember, David. *Please.*"

"No, you didn't hurt me." What hurt was the effort he'd exerted to keep from turning his lips into the palm of her hand, as she had done to his earlier. Or finding her mouth again. Or using his lips to explore not only her mouth, but the full breasts that were only a heartbeat away.

Her hand remained where it was. "David, you have to try to understand. I've had nightmares for so long. And now, today, in this of all places, the dream was so real, and so good. For once, it even had—" She broke off.

"What, Karen?"

She took a deep breath, remembering the kiss that had seemed so real. "A happy ending."

"You were dreaming about Tim."

She bit her lip, knowing she couldn't tell him that when she had first regained consciousness, the dream had been about her present and future, not the past. "I was dreaming about good times," she finally said. "Your touch only seemed to reinforce it all. And then I woke up." She wouldn't mention the kiss; she couldn't. She could tell it caused him pain, pain that was a mirror image of her own misery. She took a deep breath. "And I guess I realized that the dream was never going to come true, that the ending—the past—was never going to change." *Nor the future*, she added silently. "I wish I hadn't dreamt it at all. Oh, David, I wasn't reacting to your face. I'm sorry if I hurt you. I didn't mean to."

"I know that now. Why did you agree to come here today if you knew it was going to cause you such pain?"

Her hand fell back into her lap. "Ever since Tim's death I've stayed away from heights, and from high assignments. But I thought I could handle it today, I really did. And since I'd badgered you into agreeing to go, I wasn't about to tell you I didn't like your choice of location. I'm sorry I ruined your day." She sighed, her words muffled against his chest.

"You didn't ruin my day. I didn't really have much in the way of expectations, I guess."

She winced. Her own expectations had been so high....

"But I want to know something," David was saying. "Why didn't you at least tell me about your problem with heights after Tim's death?" If only he'd known, they would never have been in this predicament. Karen would never have been in danger, or in mental anguish. And he wouldn't have had to confront, yet again, his own painful feelings of inadequacy. But there was no way he could tell her that.

Karen stiffened at his unexpectedly harsh tone. For a too-brief time she had thought she was seeing a new David Carter, a kind man with a softer, gentler side. Now she tasted bitterness, knowing that the newness was simply an illusion, part of yet another dream, or perhaps of the nightmare that had been kindled by the trip to the mountain.

"Why, Karen? Why didn't you tell me about your vertigo?"

In spite of his withdrawal from the outside world, David Carter was still nothing less than a tenacious journalist. A dog with a bone. He'd pursue a question until he got the answer he was looking for. "You haven't exactly quizzed me about my likes and dislikes, you know. Not that they're any of your business."

"We're not talking about how you like your steak, Karen. It's not exactly responsible of you to conceal something so vital," he concluded sternly.

"Sorry about that! I didn't think you'd be interested."

He was interested, all right. If she only knew how much! And then he realized that she thought he didn't care. "I would expect anyone I worked with to tell me if there was a problem like this one. Am I making myself clear?"

"Yes!" she hissed, displaying a trace of her old feistiness, as she dropped the blanket to the ground.

"Do you still want to have the picnic?" he asked, suspecting strongly that her answer would be no.

"Why not? We're here, anyway. Just don't ask me to face the drop."

"Of course not! You're sure you want to stay?" he asked, stripping off his heavy pullover and draping it around her.

"Sure." But she didn't really want to, she acknowledged to herself. She wanted to leave the mountain, never to return. But since she didn't intend to spoil things even more, she ate what little she could. Residual shock had decimated her appetite, and she had to force herself to chew even part of a chicken wing.

David had never seen her look so fragile. He watched her pick at her food. Her delicate skin was far too pale, the emerald eyes shadowed and haunted. He didn't know how to erase the physical or mental signs of her distress. He only knew that he was the cause of it all. He also feared that now she must hate him for bringing her face-to-face with her past.

In spite of David's concern, there was an undercurrent that gnawed at her. As she tried to nibble on chicken that tasted like so much sawdust, she observed him, the tight set to his mouth, the blue eyes that always seemed to be looking elsewhere, the white scars livid against his fading tan. When he did at last glance at her, she felt a chill that penetrated even the warmth of the heavy sweater he'd lent her.

David was angry, of that she was certain. Angry with her. He hadn't said anything, hadn't even raised his voice except when he'd demanded to know why she hadn't told him of her fear of heights. Since then there had been an ominous silence that made her already low spirits plunge to even greater depths. How could such a brilliant, beautiful day have ended in such unmitigated disaster?

"Dessert?" he asked, his voice disrupting her reverie.

She almost laughed at the absurd normalcy of the question. "No. Nothing else."

That didn't surprise him; she'd hardly eaten anything. "Are you okay to drive?"

He didn't even want to stay on his precious mountain with her, she realized. He couldn't wait to leave. She'd managed to destroy whatever pleasure he might have had in the day. She should have told him about her problem, even though it would have meant canceling the outing. Next time she would— No, clearly there would be no next time. Sometimes there were no second chances.

After David packed away the picnic paraphernalia with grim efficiency, Karen walked back to the car. He was behind her all the way, in case she felt faint again.

The trip down the mountain was less than spectacular, to say the least. Her hands were glued to the steering wheel, her eyes focused on the road ahead of her. She had no need to say anything to him. It had all been said on the mountain, without words. She couldn't wait to get back to his house so she could drop him off and get back home.

David didn't try to make conversation, either. For one thing, Karen was far too upset for idle chatter; a glance out of the corner of his eye showed him the tense set of her jaw and the whiteness of her knuckles as her fingers grasped the steering wheel.

When they reached his house, she smothered a sigh of relief as she put on the parking brake. "Goodbye, David."

"Do you want to come inside for a while?"

She shook her head. "No. If I made it down that mountain, I can handle twenty more miles." And she was afraid that if she spent much more time in David's company, she would break down completely.

"Call me when you get home," he ordered gruffly.

"Why?" she blurted out, startled.

"Because I want to be sure you get home all right, why else? Humor me, okay? Please," he added.

"I'll call you."

"Drive carefully," he said quietly.

"I always do," she replied. But instead of putting the car in gear and heading for home, she turned her head back toward him. "I guess this will be all the excuse you need," she said numbly.

"Excuse?"

"To give working with me the kiss of death. Now you have an easy out."

"What the hell are you talking about?"

"Oh, come on, David. I can't function in high places. That means that I obviously can't provide you with the kind of photographic support you need. Use some initiative. Pick up the phone and tell Larson he should pull somebody else for you. Or better yet—" she laughed, unaware of the edge of hysteria in the sound "—tell him that it's all off—me *and* the assignment!" With that, she drove off without a backward glance.

How long he stood there, gazing at her departing car until it became invisible, he had no idea. Why did she get to him, get under his skin? What did she really want, other than the assignment on her résumé? Or maybe this was her own way of getting out of working with him! And if that was true, why did he care?

KAREN ARRIVED HOME nearly an hour later. Her Federal Hill apartment had never looked so inviting. She took the stairs slowly, holding on to the bannister. Once inside she ran a hot bath, intending to soak until she looked like a prune. But before that she went to the phone and dialed a number she knew only too well. "I'm home," she said without preamble when he answered.

"You're all right?"

"I'm fine."

"Karen."

"Give it a rest, David. I'll bring your sweater...when I see you again. Good night." She hung up.

After her bath she put on a nightgown, crawled into bed and pulled the comforter up to her chin. She should never have meddled with his life-style, or with David himself. It was none of her business. Would she ever learn?

She wasn't sorry that sleep eluded her. She had no wish to sleep, because she had no wish to dream the kind of dream she usually did. Dreams of mountains and pain and great sadness. As she stared through the heavy darkness at the blank ceiling, her tired mind played and replayed the bitter parting words she'd spoken to David. Maybe they were the last words she would ever say to him. Because it was more than possible he would use her fear of heights against her. Toward dawn she fell into a heavy, exhausted sleep that even the blackest nightmare couldn't penetrate.

DAVID POURED HIMSELF another glass of single-malt Scotch, grimacing as the liquid burned his throat when he downed it too fast. Karen had ignored her fear of that damned mountain simply because he had wanted to go there, but not for any reason of her own. She had risked her physical and emotional well-being. It made his own fear seem paltry in comparison, or, for the first time, put it into the realm of the manageable. She hadn't told him anything beforehand, hadn't complained. She had simply endured. She had courage. What did that make him? A rank coward.

Could his fear of people's reactions to him be any worse than the terror he'd experienced, seeing her helpless—and being helpless himself to do anything about it? Racked by self-disgust, he picked up the phone, dialed a number and set in motion an event he had never thought would take place, not ever again. Once that was accomplished, he tried to sleep. When that proved impossible, he read until his eyes burned. Eventually he gave that up, too, retreating to the pool, swimming lap after lap until he could barely lever himself out and make it into bed.

8

THE SHRILL RING of the telephone jolted Karen from the depths of sleep.

"It's eight o'clock," David's voice told her.

Considering the way they'd parted the day before, she was surprised he was even calling. "If you say so," she replied coldly. "I haven't looked at my clock."

"Karen, about yesterday—"

"I don't want to talk about yesterday."

"Fine. We'll talk about today, then. Be here at ten."

Just like that, she raged inwardly. What did she expect, anyway? He probably wanted to give her her walking papers in person. "Can't you just say whatever it is you have to say on the telephone?" she asked, bracing herself for the worst.

"No," he snapped. "I need you here at ten because I've got work to do, and you're part of that work. Be here. You're still working for me, in case you've forgotten," he concluded sarcastically.

"Working for you is too uncomfortable to forget!" she retorted, almost too angry to be shocked.

"And wear something besides those combat fatigues you usually turn up in."

"Who are you to criticize what I wear?"

"Don't I get to criticize anything, Lady Photographer? You've tossed some pretty interesting words at me."

"What's the reason for dressing up?"

"Just do it!"

She got to his house ten minutes early and found him pacing in the living room, slowly and laboriously, back and forth on the crutches. "I'm here," she said as she laid the sweater he'd lent her on the sofa. When he turned toward her, she could see that his skin was almost gray with exhaustion, the scars on his face and neck even more evident than usual.

"Thank you for coming." And then he said, slowly, and for the second time, "About yesterday. . ."

"All right. About yesterday. Get it over with," she said with a sigh.

"Did you really think I'd quit? Or go to Larson and tell him that you were inadequate?"

"Don't tell me the thought never crossed your mind! And I have no idea what you're capable of doing or telling Larson. I haven't known you very long."

"And from what little you do know, that's your opinion of my character? Thanks a lot." He laughed harshly. "Well, I'm telling you now. I didn't want the damned assignment, and I didn't want to work with you. But now I'm serious about the work, and you're a part of it. I'll do the best I can. I'm not a quitter, no matter what you might think. And I never thought of asking for anyone else!"

"You never thought of asking for *me*, either!"

Silence.

"Thanks for the vote of confidence, Karen."

"I thought you'd jump at the chance to retreat to the safety of your four walls."

They haven't seemed very safe since you breached them. "Don't push it," he warned her. "I'm working on a short fuse. And I've got to be somewhere by eleven.

Are you willing to provide transportation and camera coverage?"

For a moment she simply stared at him, half believing she was only hearing things. "You're going somewhere?"

"I set up an in-person interview with Mrs. Wyatt."

"Mrs. Wyatt!" Karen echoed in shock, practically gritting her teeth in an effort to stem her rabid curiosity. What had made him change his mind? He was going to interview the woman face-to-face—something he'd said only the day before he would never do. If he'd told her this a week ago, or even the day before yesterday, she would have been over the moon and bursting with pride. Now she could barely summon the energy to sit and listen to him. It wasn't her fight. Not anymore. It never had been.

David bit back a sigh as he observed her, sitting straight and silent across from him. This was a woman he didn't know. She was polite, formal, with none of the enthusiasm he'd come to associate with her. He wondered bleakly if that Karen was gone forever, if he'd driven her away. "I want to get to know the person behind the voice on the telephone. What can you tell me? What's she really like?"

"She's a tiny, doll-like woman with a backbone of steel. She'd have to be, I suppose, to manage the corporate holdings she does. She's also not very talkative. She didn't say much when I was taking pictures last week. I was glad I wasn't doing the interviewing."

"Yeah, well, I got only 'yes' and 'no' answers out of her on the telephone. I'm hoping that talking to her in person will get better results."

Karen saw how pale David was, how he kept glancing at his watch. He was utterly and totally miserable.

If only she could do something about it. *Hold it, Karen! You've tried enough already. Too much. Stay out of it. This is his show.* She watched him pace, propelling himself the length and breadth of the living room slowly and methodically, the dual thuds of the crutches in counterpoint to his steps. It was a relief when he got into the car.

Halfway there, Karen realized that not only had he stopped moving, he was virtually frozen in place. She pulled off onto the shoulder of the road, unable to stand it any longer.

"What's wrong?" he asked.

"Nothing."

"Then why are we stopping?"

She gazed at him intently. "Why do you think?" She could almost smell the fear in him. She turned to him, laying her hand on the tightly bunched muscles of his forearm in what she meant as a gesture of reassurance.

Instinctively his strong fingers reached out to cover hers, not letting go.

"Tell me what's wrong."

"Fear," he admitted starkly.

"Give me a worst-case scenario."

"She'll be repelled—not let me in—"

"More likely she won't let you out! In spite of her considerable wealth, I think Mrs. Wyatt's lonely. Maybe she'll open up to you. Try to relax. You're stiff as a board."

"Thanks for the pep talk."

When Karen pulled up to Mrs. Wyatt's yellow-brick mansion, David got out of the car with no more diffi-culty than usual. The doorbell was answered by a petite woman with white hair, who immediately welcomed Karen back.

"It's so nice to see you again, Ms Anderson. And you must be David Carter," Mrs. Wyatt continued, extending a blue-veined hand to the man on crutches who towered over her.

Bracing himself, David took the woman's hand. "It's a pleasure to meet you, Mrs. Wyatt."

During the interview that followed, Karen saw an entirely different David Carter. For the first time she was seeing the reporter in action. She admired the way he put Mrs. Wyatt at ease, asking about her prominently displayed collection of china and crystal ornaments, walking through her library, complimenting her on the formal gardens outside.

He wasn't aggressive, didn't press for answers, was very laid back. He would ask one question; Mrs. Wyatt would respond with a paragraph of answers. David's pen scribbled across the pages of his slender reporter's notebook. But Karen could tell that a great deal of the raw material of the interview wasn't on paper yet; it was in his head.

Evidently the day had taken its toll, Karen realized as she matched her steps to David's much slower ones on the way back to the car later. It was as if a light had been switched off, as if the man who now walked laboriously beside her was a mere ghost of the one who had interviewed Mrs. Wyatt with such consummate skill. When they reached the car, she opened the door for him. It was a measure of his extreme weariness that he let her take the crutches from him after he'd seated himself. He said nothing on the way back. And she respected his silence.

Once back in the house, Karen expected that David would immediately head for his typewriter to begin integrating today's notes with what he'd already written.

There was no need for her to be there; she told him as much.

"I disagree. You read the first version. I'd like some feedback on the second. But first, lunch. I don't know about you, but I haven't eaten much in the last day or so. All right with you?"

"My time is your time," she replied curtly.

In an atmosphere of uncomfortable silence, they ate ham-and-cheese sandwiches in the kitchen. To Karen, it was almost a reprise of the disastrous picnic on Sugar Loaf Mountain. The food was tasteless. Maybe one of the side effects of this assignment would be a loss of appetite.

Afterward, David spent two hours in his office, determined to reconcile his first draft with the day's notes. He should have been feeling on top of the world. After all, he'd finally dredged up the courage for a face-to-face interview. It had gone well. The resulting article would yield decent results; experience told him that. But instead of feeling hugely elated, he was possessed by an almost ridiculous sense of anticlimax. The event he had feared for so long had come and gone almost unnoticed. What really concerned him was the rift with Karen, and the fear that perhaps it couldn't be mended. It was a rift he had made, and one only he could fix.

When he finally finished the piece, it gave him no sense of pleasure and no sense of accomplishment. He pulled the last page out of the typewriter and went to give it to Karen. He found her curled up in the armchair, an open book in her lap. She wasn't reading.

"Is it ready yet?" she asked as he walked slowly toward her.

"Yes, but I want to talk to you first," he said, sitting down on the sofa.

Here it comes: "Get lost, Karen." "I'm listening."

"Could you put the book down?"

She set it back on the shelf.

"And come closer."

Smothering a sigh, she went to sit at the opposite end of the sofa. "Any other directions?"

"About yesterday."

"Enough, already. I thought we agreed that yesterday was history."

"You agreed—I didn't. I just went along for the ride. Do you really think I'd ask Larson to replace you with someone else? That I'd stoop that low?"

"I don't know. And I'm not sure if I really care anymore. For reasons that I don't even understand, I've been interfering in your well-ordered life. I know now that I had absolutely no right to do that. It won't happen again. If you decide not to call Larson, I'll go on working with you, but only on a professional basis."

"What do you mean? We've always worked together on a professional basis!"

"I mean no lunches and dinners, no swimming at the David Carter Country Club. I'm not here for that. I'll take the pictures, review them with you and drive you where you need to go if you intend to do more in-person interviews—"

"Yes, I do intend to do them!" he cut in.

"Fine," she replied smoothly. "And as for the rest—well, you go your way, and I'll go mine. And I'm sure that'll be best for both of us."

"Why?"

"Why? Because it's bad enough dealing with your anger when it's out in the open. But yesterday it was coming at me in tidal waves!"

"What are you talking about?"

"I'm talking about our little trip up to Sugar Loaf Mountain. And after I did my little swan dive, you were so helpful. You didn't let me just lie there unconscious. But afterward, during the picnic and the ride back down, you said nothing. The silence cut through me like a knife. Frankly, life's too short, David."

"You don't understand."

"Why don't you explain it, then?"

"I wasn't angry at you. I was angry at myself, because I wasn't capable of doing anything for you and I was too damned insensitive to pick up vibrations of fear from you on the way up there. All I could think of was my own damned pleasure. I guess what I'm trying to do is apologize—and hope that you believe I mean it."

She searched his face, taking note of the intense, waiting expression in his blue eyes, trying to decipher the meaning behind the words. She wanted it to be as it had been before. But she didn't think that was possible. "You said you wanted me to read the Wyatt piece...."

He winced at the coldly polite, formal tone of her voice. She didn't believe him and couldn't accept his apology. He could tell that. She had looked at him briefly, then away. He felt a deep pain, as if something he cared for had died, knowing that he had killed it. The pain increased until it became physical, a dull pounding in his head. He pulled the article from his pocket, tossing it toward Karen, then sinking back against the sofa. He was startled to see her get up. "Where are you going? I thought you were going to read the piece."

"I'd rather read it in your office, if you don't mind." She didn't want him watching her like a hawk.

"Be my guest."

With feigned indifference, she deliberately ignored him as she walked out of the living room. She felt an odd combination of intimacy and presumption as she sat in the chair at his desk. This was where he did his thinking, his writing. It was as if he were in her darkroom at home, looking at her drying negatives or the wet prints that lay in the developing tanks. She forced herself to concentrate on the article, half afraid it wouldn't be better than his first effort and wondering what she would tell him. One thing was certain: whatever she told him, it would be the truth, uninfluenced by his anxiety or her own feelings.

She needn't have worried. It was good, and written with the same flair and crisp, vibrant style that had characterized his street reporting. She put the sheets back together. He would want to know her opinion. Now.

When she came into the living room, his name was on her lips, but he wasn't there. She had a sense of déjà vu as she went to look for him, wondering if she would find him in the pool. She found him in the bedroom, sitting on the side of the bed, head bent, face in his hands. As she stood there uncertainly, watching him, she saw him rake one hand through his already disordered hair. "David?" she called softly.

He dropped his hands, immediately turning to face her. "How was it?"

"Good. It breathes. I love it, and so will Larson."

"Thanks," he said. He saw that she was hovering in the doorway, looking ready to go. "You're leaving." It was a statement, not a question.

"I'll see you tomorrow. You said the next interview would be—"

"Face-to-face?" he concluded for her. "Yes."

"Fine. Why don't you let me know when it's set up. Meanwhile I'll work on today's photos, and I'll give you a call when they're ready." *That's it*, she told herself. *Be calm. Cool. Collected. Keep those emotions fenced in, at least long enough to get out the front door!*

She paused, looked back at him and saw him massaging the back of his head as if it hurt. *Keep on walking*, she ordered herself. *Just put one foot in front of the other. The man is not your responsibility. He doesn't want your help, or need it. Nor would he thank you for offering it gratis.*

She can't wait to leave, he told himself with a sigh. As the pounding in his head crescendoed, he wished she hadn't been in such a hurry; he would gladly have traded a Pulitzer Prize for an aspirin. He flicked a disgusted glance at the crutches. The bathroom medicine cabinet had never seemed so far away. He cocked his head, heard Karen's muffled footsteps as she walked down the hallway to the living room, where she would soon reach the front door. And made a split-second decision.

Her hand was on the strap of her heavy gadget bag when she heard her name being called. She set the bag down on the floor and walked back to his room in time to see him again lifting a hand to the back of his head. "Yes?"

"Can you get me a couple of aspirins and some water?"

She concentrated on hiding her shock. He had never before asked her for anything, had never willingly betrayed any vulnerability, had never acknowledged needing any help. "Sure," she said with a nod, then left to get him what he'd asked for. When she came back into the room, she walked briskly toward him, intending to drop the pills into his outstretched hand and leave. His hand was shaking. As she shook the pills into his palm, she fought to keep her own hand from shaking as well.

"Thanks," he said after swallowing the pills and washing them down with the water.

"Headache?"

He shrugged resignedly. "It's probably from tension and lack of sleep. I spent a lot of last night swimming laps and trying to work the kinks out." The fingers of one large hand massaged his temples as if that could ease the tightness that seemed to be getting worse.

An impulse surfaced, urging her to his side. Another, more sensible voice advised her to back away before his behavior hit a new low. Karen told the sensible voice to shut up. "Is it bad?" she asked him as she saw that his jaw was clenched and his eyes were narrowed with pain.

"It'll pass."

"I have an idea that might be better than aspirin," Karen said diffidently, feeling rather like a fool.

"I don't know what you mean," he said, looking up at her.

She took a deep breath, then went to stand in front of him, placing her fingers very lightly at his temples. When he stiffened, she withdrew her touch immediately. "I didn't mean to startle you."

"You didn't." How could he tell her that the mere touch of her soft hands—and the proximity of her breasts—were wreaking havoc with his nervous system? "What—what were you going to do?"

"Just practice a little something I read about in the *Met*'s health section."

For a long moment he held himself very still. Then: "It can't hurt to try it, I guess. What do I have to do?"

"Just turn toward the window."

"Turn toward the window," he echoed. And away from her, he added silently, smothering a groan of frustration that left his hands balled into fists. "Now what?"

She said nothing further, but placed her fingers once more at his temples and began a slow, circular motion, moving gingerly as her fingers encountered the jagged scar.

He closed his eyes as the almost hypnotic movements began, luxuriating in the sensations she was creating. He allowed his head to move back and forth with the motions of her hands.

Her fingers traveled past his temples, working through the crisp silkiness of his hair to the scalp underneath. Each time, her touch found him tense under her hands. Then, very gradually, she could feel the tension ease away, as if it were flowing from his taut muscles into her kneading fingers.

As his muscles gradually relaxed, she was gratified to see that his breathing evened, the clenched fists at his sides loosened and his head fell back against her hands, almost like a caress. Very gradually she moved her fingers to the back of his head, then lower to the tightly knotted muscles of his neck and shoulders.

She looked down at his face, saw that the furrows of pain at his mouth had relaxed, that his eyes were half-closed, then saw the thick, black lashes that, lowered, fanned into crescents. A groan of what seemed like pure pleasure was wrung from him as his head, which seemed much heavier now that some of the tension had left him, came to rest against the softness of her breast.

Her hands stilled abruptly as she fought for breath. She dropped her hands, resisting the urge to press her lips to the crown of his head.

"Karen?" The absence of her touch was almost a physical pain.

"Could you...lie down, please?" she asked when she could finally speak, praying that her voice held a measure of steadiness.

"On my back or face down?" he asked matter-of-factly, all the while relieved that she wasn't leaving—at least, not yet.

"Face down."

Without another word, without asking why, he turned the comforter back and edged toward the center of the bed so there would be room for her. Then he lay down on his stomach, pillowing his head on his crossed arms.

Once more she began to massage his temples and scalp. She shifted her hands to his heavily muscled shoulders, each movement she made a kind of caress that came from her heart. She stifled the urge to smooth the hair she herself had ruffled, to soothe it with her lips, to know its softness. He wouldn't appreciate the gesture; he wasn't interested in her that way. Slowly, gradually, she heard the even tenor of his breathing, and knew that it was past time for her to leave.

"How do you feel?" she asked.

"Better. Much better. Not from the aspirin. Magic hands," he murmured, eyes closed, his voice blurred as if he were just on the edge of sleep.

"Thanks," she replied in what she hoped was the manner of a professional masseuse. "All you need now is to get some rest."

"I think I'm half asleep now," he said with a sigh.

"Right. I'm not exactly wide awake myself."

"Damn!"

"What is it, David?"

"I know you must want to leave."

She removed her hands immediately. "Whatever you say."

He flipped over onto his back, immediately latching on to her left wrist. "It's not that I want you to go." He reddened slightly with the admission. "It's just that I feel guilty. You must be as tired as I am."

She was touched by his concern. "I'll survive."

"Please stay, at least for a while."

"Oh, David—"

"I have a good reason for asking you to stay," he said quickly, hoping to persuade her. "I don't want you driving home in a state of exhaustion."

"All right. I'll stretch out on the sofa for a while."

"What's wrong with stretching out here?" he asked with deceptive softness.

"Here?" she echoed. As in, on his bed—next to him? "Next to you?"

"Next to me. There's nobody else here that I know of. The bed's a king-size," he stated casually. "There's plenty of room. And it would certainly be more comfortable for you than the sofa."

"All right," Karen said hesitantly as she walked around to the far side of the bed, piled a couple of pillows against the headboard and lay down on top of the comforter.

The silence between them stretched uncomfortably, until David's voice broke it.

"Karen, I'd like to ask you something."

"About what?"

"About something you said on Sugar Loaf Mountain."

"Oh, please, no more!" she protested. "I want to forget all that."

"There was something you said," he continued stubbornly.

"I said a lot of things."

He bit back a retort. "When I asked you why you'd never told me about your fear of heights, you said I'd never asked about your likes and dislikes. Well, I'm asking now."

She propped herself against the pillows, looking down at him blankly. "Why now?"

"I've been pretty self-centered," he admitted, his mouth twisting in a wry grin. "I guess I still am," he said, more to himself than to her, "always considering my problems to be unique and insurmountable. Well, since you, er, came into my life, so to speak, my focus has kind of changed. I didn't even realize how much until yesterday. Tell me something about Karen Anderson. Please."

"There's not much to tell. I mean, you're an international journalist, and I'm just a general-assignment photographer."

"And working with me is a pretty tough general assignment. Come on, lady. Give. Or I'll have to dream up a background for you. Let's see, you were born with a camera in your hand. . . ."

"All right, all right." She laughed ruefully. "I guess I'd better come up with something before you create a fictionalized version of everything. I became hooked on photography when my father gave me my first camera on my tenth birthday. I've worked on local and regional papers, as well as doing free-lance work. I still free-lance, and of course, I work at the *Met*."

"That sounds like the bare essentials. You could find out the same kind of stuff about me by reading my sketch file in the *Met* library." When his comment was greeted by an uneasy silence, he glanced at the woman lying stiffly beside him, and saw that she was blushing. "You did read it, didn't you?" he asked softly.

"Larson had me read your files before I even went to meet you."

"And what did you find out?"

"Just the basics—that you're thirty-four, served time working on a couple of small-town papers in the Carolinas before you came to the *Met*." She wasn't about to tell him that she'd learned much more than that from Mickie Lewin—or that she'd seen the photograph in *Metro-Lights*. "Among other things," she added nonchalantly, "I didn't need to read through your entire clipping file to figure out that you were a dynamite writer."

"One that you were just dying to work with." He laughed shortly.

"So sue me." She shrugged, amazed to see a trace of red outlining his cheekbones. David obviously wasn't all that used to compliments!

"All right, never mind me. Tell me more about you." When she hesitated, he fixed her with what he hoped was a reproachful stare. "You can consider this a practice session for my upcoming face-to-face interviews."

"Oh, all right." She sighed. "I like almost any kind of food."

"Tell me something I don't know. I don't even know how old you are or where you live."

She smothered a giggle, telling him that she was twenty-eight, lived in a second-floor Federal Hill apartment, liked all kinds of music from Mozart to Marsalis, as well as novels with happy endings. She enjoyed crabbing on the Chesapeake Bay with her father, her mother's cooking and baseball better than football....

"And you love swimming."

"Yes."

"Will you tell me now why you swim with such desperation? Why you push yourself so hard?"

She drew away from him, knowing that to say the words, she would have to compose herself, and that would be hard. "I swim for the same reason that some people drink—to forget. When I'm lucky and I get tired enough, I come home and sleep the night through."

"Instead of having nightmares about falling and mountains," he said softly.

"Yes. I think I'd better leave now." So many things had been said, so many painful things. To her surprise, his fingers reached over to grasp her wrist.

"Don't go," he murmured huskily.

"I'm tired, David. I really am."

She was also very tense. He could feel it. "I know you are."

"So are you," she added, seeing that his blue eyes were barely open. "My autobiography practically put you to sleep."

"Lie down again," he urged, not taking his eyes or his hand from her. "There's plenty of room. You really shouldn't drive when you're this tired."

"I don't think I'll sleep."

"You can rest your eyes," he coaxed. And then, aware of her underlying fear, he said very softly, "I'll be here . . . if the nightmares come."

His sensitivity brought her to the edge of tears, but before she could thank him, she saw that his eyes had closed. Very gently she removed her wrist from his lax fingers, placing his hand at his side. Then she moved the pillows and lay down at the opposite edge of the mattress, intending to stay for only a few minutes. A very few minutes.

DAVID WOKE to dark silence and the unaccustomed awareness of the tender curves and valleys of a warm, female form against the lean, hard planes of his own body. While she slept, Karen had turned toward him, unconsciously bridging the empty space that had been between them when he'd closed his eyes. Her head nestled in the hollow of his shoulder; one slender arm was curled around his waist. He wanted to take her in his arms, kiss her until her lips were love swollen and stroke her body until she vibrated with the same longing for him that he felt for her. Oh, God!

He shivered, telling himself it was from the cold. Shifting very carefully so as not to disturb Karen, he retrieved the caramel comforter from the end of the bed, pulling it over her shoulders. Then he lay down beside her again and, with a supreme effort of will, closed his eyes once more, hoping to delay the inevitable.

For a time he lay sleepless, gritting his teeth as he maintained a position that was heartbreakingly near— and agonizingly far. And then he felt her stir beside him. A touch of his hand revealed a light sheen of moisture on the downy softness of her skin. It needed only the heartbreaking little moans escaping from her throat for him to draw her into his arms.

"It's all right, sweetheart," he crooned, desperately wishing he had the right to guard her against the nightmares every night. With the touch of a butterfly on a delicate flower, his lips drank the salty moisture from her skin, then came to rest in the scented tangle of her hair. "It's all right, sweetheart. Sleep."

KAREN AWOKE some time later, puzzled to find an unaccustomed weight across her breasts. David's arm. When she tried to ease away from him, the arm moved. He shifted in his sleep, and his arm found its way to her waist, where it settled. Where it felt so right. Why was it that she had avoided the touch of men for so long but was so reluctant to stray from this man's nearness?

The answer, when it came, was so startling that she almost sat bolt upright. Inwardly she was shaking. When had it happened, this strange feeling for David Carter? Today, just now, with her fingers giving him sweet solace, his head heavy on her breast? Or on the mountain, when she'd lain insensible in his arms, later awaking to find her mouth fused to his? Or was it that rainy night when she had first seen his pain, inside and out? Oh, God. She loved him—*loved* him—this complex, difficult man. She who hadn't thought anyone could supplant Tim in her heart. Now she had found that there was room in her heart for David, as well. His own place. If he wanted to be there. Which she very much doubted. Somehow she managed to slide out from under his arms without waking him. She pulled up the heavy velvet comforter, covered him and made her escape.

WHEN DAVID AWOKE for the second time, he felt only the weight of the comforter. He flipped it back, disturbed by the odd feelings that descended on him all at once. The only one he could read clearly was loneliness.

Once he'd made his way to the dresser, he read the yellow note she'd attached to the first page of his article.

David,
Thanks for standing guard.
See you in the morning.

The scrap of paper with her three-line note meant more to him than the whole article he'd worked so hard to create.

9

AFTER THE WYATT INTERVIEWS, nothing was quite the same. It seemed like there was an interview almost every day, as well as travel that took them all over the state. They went to Southern Maryland to look at a school for merchant seamen, to Salisbury to see a chicken factory in production, and to Gaithersburg, to see the results of the governor's efforts to introduce high tech to the East Coast. And they went to Columbia, to see yet another attempt at planned community living. And there were two more Worthington Valley pieces, including a humorous one with the head of the local basseting group. Basseting, Karen was amused to find, was a unique local sport. It involved groups of dedicated walkers tramping over hill and dale in the wake of a pack of slow-moving basset hounds—which never managed to catch a very swift rabbit.

As the interviews progressed, Karen began to notice subtle changes in her relationship with David. He often had coffee and doughnuts waiting for her when she was due to arrive in the morning. And he seemed to assume she would eat dinner at his house at the end of the day. Sometimes he cooked; other times she brought food with her and cooked it there. And more than once they sent out for double-crust, double-cheese pizzas with everything on them.

On weekends, when work wasn't heaviest, Karen found she enjoyed spending a Saturday evening in front of David's big stone fireplace, with Bach and Beethoven and their contemporaries in the background. Sunday mornings were often spent in a joint assault on the *Times* crossword puzzle, Karen teasing David about getting involved with a rival paper. And sometimes, in the car to and from interviews, or late at night until whenever in the morning, they just sat and talked about everything and nothing.

It was almost as if they were an old married couple, Karen thought to herself more than once, except that she sensed that David never seemed to want to get close to her. And although they talked of almost everything under the sun, one word never entered the conversation: love.

Her love—the love she had acknowledged for the first time the day of the Wyatt interview—remained her secret. It manifested itself in the things she did for him and in the pleasure she took in just being near him. She would have given anything to be able to go to him and say, "David, I love you," but she held back, instinctively fearing he wasn't ready for that—might never be ready for it.

And even though the coldness and remoteness were gone, she sensed a wariness in him that was never too far from the surface. Even during their comfortable evenings together he would sit at one end of the sofa, she at the other end, or in a chair, or in a nest of cushions. But not too close to him. So she took her love, placed it carefully in an imaginary box and nurtured it with the sense of well-being that she derived from being with him every day. Someday, she hoped devoutly, she would be able to take that box, open it and present him with the gift of her love.

She was simply amazed at the amount of work he could turn out when he put his mind to it—and at the way he expected her to keep up with the killing pace he set. The days were long and tiring, but satisfying, nonetheless. Never had she felt so committed to a project, so part of a team effort. And, surprise of surprises, she managed to sleep whole nights without the nightmares that had tormented her for so long. She was that tired by the time the long days finally drew to an end.

Since she couldn't tell David of her love, she tried to be there for him, supportive in all possible ways. Because she knew he wasn't at ease in the interview process yet. And certainly not every person he talked to was a Mrs. Wyatt!

Karen was proud of David, but she hated the looks he sometimes received, realizing that her note of so long ago had been quite naive. Not everyone looked at him as she did, seeing the inside as well as the outside. But he seemed to be adjusting to it. Sometimes he even managed to laugh about it.

A case in point was the overheard conversation, much too loudly spoken, at a filling station where they'd stopped for gas on the way back to Baltimore after an interview. One of the attendants washed the windows, while another checked the oil. Then, one man shook his head and said, "What the hell does she see in him? He must be rich." And Karen, whose temper was never far from the surface in situations like that, was unable to stop herself from retorting, "He's not rich. He's sexy!"

At first, she thought she'd gone too far. She held her breath as she pulled out of the gas station. She glanced over at David, apprehensive about his reaction. His shoulders were shaking, and for a moment she was scared. Until she heard his shout of laughter.

"Oh, Karen, I can't stand it!" he gasped. "You're priceless. Sexy!"

The trouble was, she really *did* think he was sexy. There was something about the way he moved, even with the crutches, and unfettered in the swimming pool, powerful muscles gleaming under the indoor lights. And now, since he'd gone back to work, at least on this one assignment, she was seeing some of the dynamism that had leaped out at her from the photograph in *Metro-Lights*. There was no longer emptiness in those blue eyes. . . .

"Hey, lady, you're not listening to me," David growled as he gave Karen's French braid a sharp tug to get her attention.

"Did I miss something?" she asked innocently.

"Yeah. You missed something. I was wondering if you think this sexy reporter will wow 'em at the Spiceco shareholders' meeting tomorrow?"

Which started the laughter all over again.

David was to interview Gregory Martin, the president and chief executive officer of the Maryland-based spice company that had just gone public. After Karen parked her car on the lot near the company's main building, she and David made their way to the reception area, where a svelte brunette, who was sitting at the desk, just barely managed to smother a gasp of shock as she looked up and saw the man coming through the door.

"C-can I help you?" the woman finally managed.

"I'm David Carter, from the *Metropolitan*," he said, forcing himself to ignore the expression on the woman's face. "I'm here to interview Mr. Martin."

The receptionist seemed only too happy to usher the two visitors into her boss's august presence.

Karen held her breath, expecting the worst. But the man came out from behind his desk, offered his hand in greeting and invited both his visitors to be seated.

"I'm sorry I can only give you a small amount of time before the shareholders' meeting. But feel free to join us for lunch in the staff dining room. All the company officials will be there. Ask all the questions you want, except for trade secrets, of course." He laughed drily.

So far so good, Karen thought with a mental sigh of relief, wondering what David would do when confronted with a roomful of strangers. But talk about anticlimax—when he finally entered the meeting room, nobody paid him any attention at all. All the shareholders were too busy collecting their burgundy-canvas gift packages or talking among themselves about the proposed stock split.

"Check this out," David said.

She looked up at him questioningly as he handed her a glossy publication.

"It's their in-house magazine. A P.R. guy just gave it to me. Check out the title," he whispered, his unsmiling face in sharp contrast to the irrepressible twinkle she saw in his eyes.

Karen had to restrain her laughter. "I don't believe it!" The magazine was called *Spicy Bits*! "The title makes it sound like one of those hard-boiled detective mags from the 1930s!" she whispered back.

When the meeting was over, they went to lunch in the staff cafeteria, as Gregory Martin had suggested. Karen was so absorbed in watching the parade of people pour in the door that she missed the fact that David had stiffened beside her. She wasn't aware that there was anything wrong until she felt his steel-fingered grasp on her arm. "What—" She turned just in time to see his jaw clench, and the scars turn livid. "What's wrong?" she whispered, her fingers reaching out to cover his.

"There's a woman coming toward us," he said curtly.

Karen looked up and saw a very attractive, middle-aged woman in a Chanel suit bearing down on their table. The woman's utter elegance made Karen, who was dressed in gabardine slacks and a turquoise silk blouse, feel like a grunge hound. "Do you know her?"

"I wish to hell I didn't."

Before he could say anything else, the woman had come to the table. Almost as if she were watching a movie, Karen watched David rise slowly to his feet.

"Hello, David," the woman said, her eyes seeming to rest anywhere but on his face.

If she didn't want to look at him, why had she bothered to seek him out? Karen wondered angrily.

"Hello, Mother." And then, in an undertone to Karen, "I believe I mentioned that my mother is involved in corporations."

Karen was glad she had the table to cling to. His mother, who, according to him, hadn't seen her son in more than a year, and when she *had* seen him, hadn't been able to look him in the face. David hadn't exaggerated, Karen realized, aching for him to the depths of her soul.

"Your father thinks very highly of Spiceco. I'm here at the shareholders' meeting because he's out of town and couldn't attend. Do you have shares in the company, too?" the woman asked, her voice as coldly polite as if she were speaking to a stranger.

"No, Mother. I'm here to interview Gregory Martin."

"Really. I thought you weren't doing that kind of thing anymore."

"I was out of it for a while. I'm back now."

Be glad for him, Karen urged the woman silently.

"You know where it got you before, David."

"Yes, Mother. I know. Flat on my back. Whatever happened serves me right!" he bit out between gritted teeth.

"I didn't say that, did I? But if you'd come into the family business as your father wanted, you'd be president of your own company now, not interviewing the president of this one. And you wouldn't be in this— condition. You can still come back, David. Your father is willing."

"But I'm not. Now if you'll excuse us . . ."

"Us?" the woman repeated, arching a carefully drawn brow.

"Karen Anderson is a photographer for the *Met*. Karen, this is my mother, Ellen Carter."

Karen felt a shiver run up and down her spine as the woman's blue-eyed gaze swept her from head to foot. And dismissed her just as quickly. "Miss Anderson." Ellen Carter acknowledged her with barely a nod of her carefully coiffed head before turning back to her son. "Are we to expect you to turn up some time during the Christmas holidays? You're welcome to join us, if you like."

Suddenly Karen couldn't stand it anymore. She didn't know which was worse, the man frozen in place at her side or the woman who avoided looking directly at her son. Giving David's hand a surreptitious squeeze, Karen pasted a brilliant smile on her face. "David is spending the holidays with me and my parents in Annapolis. They can't wait to meet him. We're going to have a great time. Mom and Dad always wait till I come home to trim the tree, and there's last-minute baking, and of course, carols—"

"How—quaint," Mrs. Carter replied faintly.

"I'm afraid it is." Karen laughed lightly. "And now you'll have to excuse us, Mrs. Carter. I have to get my film back to the paper for processing, and David's got an interview to finish."

"But you haven't eaten," the other woman noted, glancing down at the barely touched plates on the table.

"Oh, I never eat much, Mrs. Carter. I'm hardly ever hungry."

Karen's respect for David escalated to new heights as, moments later, she watched him conclude the in-depth interview with Gregory Martin. An outside observer might have thought everything was normal. But Karen knew differently. He sat more stiffly than usual. His fingers were curled more tightly around the gold pen he used. His speech was slightly more terse. And he expelled a long sigh of relief when the interview came to an end. A sigh that Karen heartily echoed.

"Now you see why I decided to stay with my family only as long as was absolutely necessary," he said as she headed the car back home.

"Your father is the same?"

"No, he's worse." David laughed harshly. "To hear him talk, working outside the family business is in the same league as drug pushing or industrial espionage. My father is accustomed to getting what he wants." Then he seemed to make a determined effort to shake off his somber mood. "You lie like a rug, Karen," he said in a much lighter tone.

"What does that mean?" she asked, puzzled.

"You had the gall to tell my mother you never ate much. I almost laughed out loud. And that Christmas fantasy! That was really a classic. The expression on my mother's face was wonderful. You painted such a great word picture that I almost believed what you were saying."

"Why shouldn't you? It's all true."

"I'm sure it is."

"Don't make me a liar, David."

"What do you mean?"

"Please come and spend Christmas with me and my family."

"I'm not into whopping, big celebrations. And I don't think I want to be on display for a bunch of strangers, if it's all the same to you."

"First of all, we don't have big celebrations. It's just Mom and Dad and me—and Nick," she added, concealing a smile.

"Who's Nick?" he asked gruffly.

"Oh, he's tall, dark and handsome. You'll like him."

"I—can't wait to meet him."

"Then you'll come?"

"I guess I can handle it if you can. But what about your parents?"

"You were invited for Thanksgiving." That was a sore point between them. He'd flatly refused. She was afraid he would do the same today. "The invitation still stands. Mom mentioned it just last night," Karen said, crossing her fingers against the lie. If he said yes she would call her mother as soon as she got back to her apartment.

"You're sure?"

"Positive. Oh, there's just one problem." *Nick.*

"If I'll be interfering with your social life . . ."

No matter how many times she told him, David never seemed to quite get the message that she had no real social life. She didn't bother to press the point again. "No, this is a problem that I won't be able to do anything about until you get there, and by then, it may be too late. Do you like dogs?"

He stared at her. "Dogs. Well, yes. I guess so. They seem to like me, too. An animal doesn't judge people, so it won't care that one side of my face doesn't match the other. Why?"

"We have a dog, a Labrador. He can get overly friendly. Some people don't like dogs, and I need to know if I have to put him in a kennel for the holiday."

"You'd board your dog just because of me?"

"If necessary."

"Well, it's not necessary."

10

THE RIDE TO ANNAPOLIS that Christmas Eve took little more than an hour. Karen could sense David's nervousness. She was nervous herself.

It was just after seven o'clock in the evening when the Volvo pulled up in front of the brick split-level house where her parents lived. Turning off the ignition, she breathed a silent prayer that everything would work out all right. "Let's go up to the house," she suggested. "The luggage can wait."

David was tense enough for a visit to the dentist.

"About the dog—" Karen began.

"I told you the dog wouldn't bother me. Now I suggest we get inside before we both turn into Popsicles. The wind's picking up."

From the other side of the door she heard a too-familiar sound. Barking.

"Oh, what's the use?" Karen groaned, inserting the key in the lock.

The minute the door was opened, the dog would be heading for the great outdoors, with no regard at all for the humans in its path. Karen knew what to expect, but she knew the man just behind her was in for a shock. So she moved next to him, one arm braced lightly behind his lean waist, steadying him, as the dog exploded out of the doorway and on into the fenced-in yard.

"Oh, that beast!" Dorothy Sturgis exclaimed, shaking her head. "Are you still in one piece, Karen?"

Her arm still around David's waist, Karen could feel his muscles tense at her mother's words. "No damage, Mom. How about you, David?"

"Fine," he replied hoarsely.

"Mom, this is David Carter. David, my mother, Dorothy Sturgis."

David swallowed hard. "My pleasure, Mrs. Sturgis."

"Welcome, David," Mrs. Sturgis said, extending her hand to the man with the scarred face as she looked straight into his eyes. And smiled.

David took her hand, at the same time registering the steady gaze that held a combination of shock overlaid with compassion. And smiled back.

Karen smothered a sigh of relief.

David finally made it into the house, followed by Karen. Bringing up the rear was the very large Labrador retriever who had finally returned from the cold.

"What's his name?" David asked when the front door closed.

"Nick," was Karen's reply.

"Why don't you take David's coat, dear? There's food in the kitchen if you children are hungry."

"Karen's always hungry."

"Thanks, David. You only say that because you know it's true," she replied cheerfully as she helped him off with his coat. "But as it happens, we had dinner at David's house in Baltimore. The next thing on our agenda is decorating the Christmas tree."

"It is?" he asked.

"You bet," she replied with a grin.

"Who's Nick named after, Karen?"

"His full name is Czar Nicholas the Second. You can see why it was shortened."

"Oh, I can see that all right. I'm just trying to reconcile the dog with the Nick that you said was tall, dark and handsome."

"I can't help it if you misunderstood," she said, her heart warmed by David's snort of laughter. "We rescued Nick from a snow drift at the side of the road when he was a puppy. Did you think he was a human, not a canine friend?"

"I thought exactly what you meant me to think, and you know it, lady!"

"I wish I could say that I'm sorry, but I cannot tell a lie. You're always so serious about not wanting to disrupt my nonexistent social life that I just couldn't resist the impulse. Nick and I really do have a lot of fun when I come home, even if the conversation *is* all on my side. And besides, if he put his front paws on your shoulders, as he does on mine, you'd see how tall he can be."

"Right, and being a black dog, he *is* dark, and of course, quite a handsome animal," he concluded, shaking his head. "I really fell into that one, didn't I? And you just couldn't help pulling my leg, huh?"

"Bad, David," she said, producing an appreciative groan at his ability to laugh at himself.

"Any food left, Karen?" Bill Sturgis asked as he entered the hallway.

"Oh, brother. Yes, Dad. I haven't scarfed it all up." Her father, Bill Sturgis, was tall, though not so tall as David, with a head of gray hair that was just starting to thin at the top. She made the introductions and watched as each man took the other's measure.

Afterward she and David adjourned to the living room. There was a fire in the fireplace, and a lovely blue spruce waiting in the corner. To Karen, everything was perfect.

To David, the room was utter chaos. There were boxes of ornaments, packages of tinsel and decorations strewn everywhere—and heaven only knew what else Karen had up her sleeve. The dog lay in front of the fireplace, his head on his paws. Soon Karen herself was sitting on the floor, rummaging through everything.

During the next hour and more, David helped hang ornaments. Each decoration came with its own story, he found. But instead of looking at the tiny, delicate objects Karen held in her hands, he found himself focusing on the woman herself. He marveled at the way her face changed as she told of the crystal star handed down from her Swedish great-grandmother, or the Santa and sleigh painstakingly carved by her father.

"Where are you going?" he asked once all the boxes had been closed.

"In search of my camera, of course. I take a picture of the finished product every year, you know," she informed him in mock serious tones. "It's one of my assigned tasks, just as Mom is chief cook and bottle washer and Dad is comptroller of the eggnog. Don't go away."

"Perish the thought," he muttered, leaning forward in the chair so that he could reach down and caress the dog, who lay so quietly at his feet. "I'm too exhausted to move."

Karen's only response was an impolite guffaw.

Moments later she was back, Nikon around her neck, light meter in hand. Finally, once she was satisfied with the readings, she took several shots of the beautifully decorated tree. One was a long shot, from the doorway of the living room, the others from closer vantage points. And then she came to an abrupt stop.

"Something wrong with the camera?" David asked at her worried expression.

"No. I, well—never mind." She sighed, putting the cap over the lens.

"What is it?"

"I wanted to take one more picture."

"All right. What's the problem?"

"I—I wanted to take a picture of Nick."

"Nick." David looked down at the dog, whose snout was resting across the tops of his shoes. "Oh. Well, I'll just get out of your way," he said, grasping the arms of the chair so as to lever himself out of its comfortable depths.

"No!"

David—and Nick—both looked up at Karen. David sank back into the chair, waiting. And Nick, in his doggy way, wondered what rule he'd broken *this* time. "You want Nick to move, I take it?" David suggested helpfully.

"No." Karen suddenly felt very foolish. "I, um, from a composition standpoint, it's such a good picture that I could hardly resist."

"What's a good picture?" David inquired patiently, feeling as if he were a dentist searching for the right tooth to pull.

"You and Nick and the tree," she blurted out. "It looks almost as if the scene were put together by Norman Rockwell."

"And you wanted to preserve this masterpiece for posterity, hmm?"

"Yes."

"What's stopping you, then?"

A six-foot-two stumbling block, she could have replied, but didn't. "I haven't forgotten the first time I
took your picture," she muttered.

"Neither have I!"

Karen winced at the certain knowledge that he was
remembering that other picture, and at the pain it had
caused him. Suddenly all she wanted was to get out and
away from it all, even from David. "I'm going to take
Nick for a walk," she said huskily. "I'll—see you later."

"Karen."

The word—her name on his lips—stopped her in her
tracks. "What is it?"

"I don't remember you asking me if I wanted to have
my picture taken."

"It was just an impulse. A bad one."

"Karen, didn't you ever want to be asked something,
even if you knew that the answer you were going to give
was no?"

Her slender fingers tightened on the camera. He
wanted to be asked, she mused, wondering why she was
going through this particular charade. "Mr. Carter,"
she began in formal tones, "I would very much like to
include your likeness, along with that of my dog, in my
photographic portrait of this year's Christmas tree. I
eagerly await your response."

"Yes."

If the camera hadn't been hanging from her neck, she
would have dropped it. "Yes?"

"Unless you've changed your mind. You'll have to tell
me how to, er, pose. I never have been much for going
in front of a camera, even . . . before."

He was leaning forward, his long fingers stroking the
dog's silky ears. The image would include only a few
branches of the glittery tree. But somehow, none of that

mattered. The important thing was the man sitting not in the dark, but in the light. "I like you just the way you are," she said softly, the words coming from the depths of her heart and soul. And then, leaving him no time to change his mind, she peered through the viewfinder, then depressed the shutter release. "Thank you," she whispered.

The exquisite poignancy of the moment was shattered by Nick, who chose that moment to start barking hysterically. Karen shook her head ruefully, then went to let him out. When she got back David was out of the chair, waiting for her.

"Karen."

"Yes?"

"Thank *you*."

She didn't ask him what he was talking about. She already knew. "You're welcome. About this evening . . ."

"This evening?" he queried.

"We go to church at about eleven o'clock for the candlelight service."

"No problem. Nick and I will entertain each other. Maybe I can get him to tell me the things he doesn't tell you in those interesting conversations."

"You're welcome to try. He's kind of close-mouthed, though." Then, almost as an afterthought, "Would you like to come with us this evening?"

"I haven't been to church in years. And besides—"

"It's a candlelight service," she reminded him gently. "The lights in the church will range from dim to non-existent. Each person lights the candle of the person sitting next to him. There are carols. You'd like it," she said coaxingly.

"Would I?"

"Yes."

"All right."

"You mean it!"

"I always say what I mean."

THEY DROVE TO THE CHURCH in her father's big Buick, Karen sitting beside David in the back seat. And when they walked inside the church, Karen didn't ask anyone any questions; she automatically selected one of the back pews.

Karen knew that whatever else happened, she would always remember this Christmas Eve service. St. Anne's had never looked lovelier, decked as it was with red and white poinsettias, Christmas greens and a magnificent wooden Nativity scene.

But most of all she would remember the man sitting next to her, the man whose candle she lit when the time came, the man whose surprisingly good baritone voice caused more than one head to turn when carols and hymns were sung. David stayed in his seat when it was time for Communion. Karen went with her parents and said a silent prayer for the man sitting alone with a candle in the darkness.

When they arrived back home, everyone went into the kitchen for cookies and fruitcake. Afterward David caught Karen smothering a yawn. "Don't do that!" he ordered.

"What?" She looked over at him, startled.

"Start yawning. It's catching," he said, hiding a yawn behind his own hand. "I think I'll turn in, if nobody minds. Thank you all for a wonderful evening."

"Our pleasure, David," Mrs. Sturgis said as her husband nodded in agreement. "Sleep well."

When David left the room, Karen followed in his wake, going into the den to make up the sofa bed. Her father had already brought in his luggage. "Have a good night's sleep," she said when she'd finished.

"You, too."

"If you want anything, let me know."

"I'll be fine."

"If you get hungry. . ." she said, just before reaching the door.

"I'll raid the refrigerator. Your mom gave me permission."

"If Nick—"

"I'll let the dog out and in, too, and make sure that the fire screen is up and that Santa makes it back up the chimney when he comes. Good *night*, Karen!"

"Good night, David." She laughed as she shut the door behind her.

David breathed a sigh of relief at her departure. He couldn't very well tell her what it did to his nervous system to know she was sleeping peacefully only half a house away! He lay down but didn't fall asleep immediately. From behind his closed eyes, the events of the day swirled in his mind. Karen and her family had taken him into their home. Her parents were fine people. And he had even seen another Karen Anderson, one that rough-housed with a dog that was almost bigger than she was.

For Karen, the night didn't end when she said goodnight to David. She and her mother sat up for nearly an hour and a half more, wrapping gifts and putting them under the tree.

"What do you think of him?" Karen asked.

"So far, I like him. Of course, he's on the quiet side. As for his face, well, it's not as bad as I thought it would be."

Karen nodded, not bothering to hide a smile of pure pleasure as she recalled the way David had seemed to adapt to her parents. He hadn't been on his home turf, protected by a list of questions and a spiral notebook. He'd been stripped defenseless. And to her heartfelt relief, he'd done very well. "I think David sees himself as he was when his injuries first happened." *And through the eyes of the bitch who dumped him when he was flat on his back*, she added silently. "I can't seem to make him realize that he needs to see a new reflection of himself in his mirror."

"Does he realize that you're looking at him with love in *your* eyes, dear?"

Karen bent her head, her attention focused on a pile of tangled ribbon. "Does it show, Mom?"

"Put it down to maternal instinct. When are you going to tell David?"

"I don't know when, or even how. For now, all I'm doing is taking one step at a time...."

WHEN KAREN GOT UP the next morning, the first thing she did was feed the dog and let him out. Then she had her morning shower and dressed in gray wool slacks and a winter-white Shetland sweater. Nobody in the Sturgis household dressed up for exchanging presents.

She let Nick back into the house, then went quietly into the den to wake David. He was sprawled on his stomach, the smoothly muscled expanse of his back exposed; the tangle of blanket and sheets barely covered his lean hips. His dark brown hair was ruffled, the often stern lines of his face were relaxed in sleep. She sat down cross-legged on the floor next to the bed and very softly called his name.

"Mmmph," was his only reply. Not even an eyelash fluttered.

Try again, Karen, she told herself, thinking how much like a little boy he looked, and just as unwilling to wake up. This time she reached up to touch the exposed arm nearest her. "David."

A gentle groan, and all of a sudden he was no longer passive; his hand was holding hers.

"'Morning. Is there some reason why you decided to wake me from the best night's sleep I've had in years?" he grumbled, his eyes barely open.

"Good morning. Everyone opens presents together," she informed him smartly. "Juice, coffee and toast in the kitchen first. Then we adjourn to the living room for the goodies. Now get cracking, lazy!" And before he could say anything else, she was up and gone.

Half an hour later everyone was assembled in the living room, no one looking terribly awake.

"It's Karen's turn to be Santa," Bill Sturgis said.

"It's been my turn since I was old enough to read the package labels!" But she laughed good naturedly.

The first presents to be delivered were the stockings that had been hung by the chimney. To David's surprise, she laid a stocking in his lap, as well. "Me, too?"

"You're part of our Christmas family, David. We certainly couldn't have let you go stockingless!" Karen's mother told him, a twinkle in her eyes. "Go ahead. Dig in."

He found a man's handkerchief, an orange and a miniature dictionary—to help him write short stories, Karen told him laughingly. He continued examining his trophies, all the while keeping an eye on Karen as she examined her own treats, and was rewarded by the stunned expression on her face.

"Trail mix!" she gasped, turning to David, who was looking smug, his arms folded across his chest.

"I slipped it to your mother yesterday. She's always running out, Mrs. Sturgis," he said by way of explanation.

"Well, it's good to know that Karen has someone in the big city to look after her interests."

Karen hurried over to the tree to begin retrieving the presents, and to hide her blush. Imagine, she'd been taking care of herself for years. She didn't need anyone to do it for her. And even though things between David and her had been better lately, the idea of his watching out for her was a shocker.

"What's the holdup?" her father asked. "You looking for the presents at the North Pole?"

"Made a wrong turn at Alaska," she muttered, grabbing several packages and handing them around.

As usual, there were clothes, high-tech gadgets and games like Trivial Pursuit. Karen gave her father a pair of gold-anchor cuff links, knowing that, having been in the Navy, he had a love for all things nautical. For her mother, she'd selected a deep-blue, velvet robe with gold braid trim. From her parents Karen herself received the new digital recording of Vivaldi's *Four Seasons*, as well as a new CD player.

Her parents were particularly delighted with David's presents. He'd managed to come up with a bottle of Chivas Regal for her father, and several spy thrillers for her mother. And for her, well, Karen was sorry she couldn't have opened the velvet jeweler's box in private.

When it had first emerged from the wrapping, she'd had the wild idea that perhaps it was a ring. That thought lasted only until her shaking fingers had managed to lift the lid, revealing an exquisitely wrought pendant, in the shape of a golden camera, its lens a single ruby. The camera was suspended from a delicate chain. "David, it's wonderful," she said, wanting more than anything to be able to fling her arms around his neck and kiss him. But she held back, seeing the expression on his face.

"I'm glad you like it."

"I love it," she corrected. "Will you put it on for me?" she asked hesitantly. At his slow nod, she sat on the floor in front of him, reaching up to hand him the box. She felt him lift her hair, then slide his fingers along the sensitive nape of her neck as he secured the chain. Then it was time for her gift to him, and she went back to the tree to retrieve the present it had taken her so long to find.

David carefully unwrapped the box Karen handed him. Lifting off the top, he pulled aside protective tissue that revealed a long-sleeved pullover of softest wool. He lifted it out of the box, loving the feel of the garment over his hands. It was so soft as to be sensual. The only thing he could imagine as more sensual would be the feel of Karen's velvet flesh against his own. Lost in his imaginings, he didn't realize she'd spoken to him until he felt the touch of her fingers on his forearm. "I— I'm sorry. I guess my thoughts were wandering."

"I asked you if you liked the sweater," she said softly, looking up at him.

"It's beautiful," he said in response, covering her fingers with his own as if it were the most natural thing in the world. *You're beautiful*, he added silently, *lovelier than anything money could buy or any man could pray for.*

"I hope it fits."

The sweater, he reminded himself with a jolt. *Keep your mind on the gift, not the giver.* "It will," he said, willing the edge of roughness from his voice. "I can't wait to put it on. Thank you."

LATE THAT AFTERNOON, Karen dressed for Christmas dinner with more than usual care. She chose a green-and-red taffeta skirt that fell in stiff folds to the floor and rustled as she walked. Her white, off-the-shoulder silk blouse had full, dolman sleeves and delicate workings of lace in the deep cuffs and in the border that edged the provocatively low V, just barely concealing the shadowy cleft between her breasts. Her hair was worn loose but gently pulled back from either side of her face with two rhinestone clips. David's gift gleamed in the hollow of her throat. The gold band, which had belonged to her in another life, she placed in her jewel box.

Karen managed to make a grand entrance, coming down the stairs to the entrance hall where her parents and David were waiting.

"You look lovely, darling," her father told her.

"Thanks, Dad," she murmured, wondering all the while why David hadn't said anything.

Unable to move or speak, David stared up at Karen as if he'd never seen her before. This Karen Anderson he didn't know. She was a woman who was lovely beyond imagining, like a brilliant butterfly emerging from a drab chrysalis. He felt her beauty almost as a physical pain. "You look . . . wonderful," he breathed as he waited for her at the base of the staircase.

"You look pretty good, too." She was delighted to note that, along with his brown wool slacks and fine camel sport jacket, he was wearing the cream-colored sweater she'd given him for Christmas.

During the sumptuous meal that was served, David was barely aware of the laden table. All he noticed was Karen sitting across from him, her face animated as she spoke.

Later that evening, as her parents went upstairs, Karen turned to David and suggested they move to the den. "I want to try out my new Vivaldi recording, if you don't mind."

"I don't mind," he assured her as he followed her out of the living room.

He lit a fire in the fireplace, while Karen adjusted the sound so that it wasn't so loud as to prohibit conversation. Some time later Mrs. Sturgis came in with a tray of hot chocolate, marshmallows and two skewers.

"Miniature sword fight?" David quipped after thanking Karen's mother for the snack.

"Marshmallows at twenty paces," Karen returned, folding back the fire screen as she settled down in front of the flames. "This is another one of our Christmas traditions," she told him, threading a marshmallow onto her skewer and holding it toward the fire. She took it out just as it got golden-toasty and ate it slowly and blissfully.

"Another?" David asked, extending his own toasted marshmallow to her, loving the way the leaping firelight turned her hair to molten gold and gave her skin an opalescent glow.

"What about you?" she asked as she nibbled at his offering.

"I'll do another one, don't worry." In reality, he was perfectly content to sit back and watch Karen's obvious enjoyment of the gooey treats.

Four marshmallows later, Karen closed the fire screen and set the cups and saucers aside. "I guess I should get out of here and let you get some sleep."

"Stay until the end of the recording," he said, reluctant to let the magical evening end.

He shouldn't be sitting on the floor that long, even though it was carpeted, Karen decided. "Only if we move to the sofa," she told him. She curled up at one end, her heart leaping as he sat down just within touching distance.

She allowed her eyes to drift shut, letting the music wash over her in waves. The end of the recording came far too soon, Karen concluded fifteen minutes later, wishing David would ask her to play it again just so that she wouldn't have to leave. She leaned back, opening her eyes slowly, and then more widely, as her gaze fastened on an object, a symbolic Sword of Damocles hanging almost directly over her head. *Thank you, Mom and Dad.* "I'll make up the bed in a minute."

"Fine. No rush." David would be content to sit there forever if she continued to sit beside him.

"But I can't until we take care of some unexpected business."

"What's that?" he asked, puzzled.

She pointed toward the ceiling. "Mom has Dad hang the stuff all over the house."

His gaze followed her hand, and saw the sprig of mistletoe suspended over their heads. And before he realized it, her arms were linked at the back of his neck, gently pulling his head toward her. Her mouth tentatively sought his, her lips just brushing his own.

He stiffened, literally unable to move, so shocked was he by her action. What followed shocked him even more.

Karen looked up into David's blue eyes. The fire-light reflects in them, she realized absently as she reached up to hold his face between her two hands.

"Karen."

She could see the uneven heaving of his chest as he endured her touch. The muscles of his jaw clenched as she traced her fingertips lightly, caressingly, over the scars that marked not only his flesh, but his life. And her lips traced the path that each furrow etched in his tightly drawn face. Without words, she told him, "It's all right. The scars don't matter."

Her kisses were like mere drops of water to a thirsty man in the parched desert. When she pulled back as if to get up, he grasped her waist, tugging gently but firmly, and drew her slowly toward him. One hand came up to cup the back of her head, fingers sifting through the golden silkiness of her hair. And then his mouth descended until it was separated from hers by a mere cushion of air.

Her arms crept up around his neck, her fingers combing through the crisp, dark hair at his nape. Strong hands framed either side of her face. She didn't know who made the final move, he or she. But suddenly they were no longer apart. First his lips, then his tongue traced and retraced the shape of her mouth until she could no longer remain passive. Her mouth opened under his, accepting his offering, her tongue dueling with his.

She felt bereft when his mouth left hers.

"Sweet," he murmured, catching her close to him. "So sweet."

"Hot chocolate and marshmallows," she murmured back, enjoying the taste of him, as well.

"Having had a taste, I could become addicted," he said with a sigh, knowing someone should call a halt. But his body seemed to want to stay exactly where it was. And hers hadn't retreated at all. If anything, she was even closer. His mouth lingered once more on hers, then sought the sensitive areas behind her ears, the delicate hollow of her throat, before descending to follow the path of the finely wrought lace as it draped over the tender curves of her breasts.

His callused hand was gentle as it traced first one breast, then the other. His lips followed, seeking her nipples through the thin layers of silk blouse and lacy bra. And then she felt him reach inside the V of her blouse, while at the same time his mouth found hers again. "David," she breathed, before words were a thing of the past.

"Karen" he muttered hoarsely, his breath coming in short, arrhythmic gasps as he pressed a quick, hard kiss to the swollen curves of her mouth. "I need to touch you."

"Yes."

She felt his fingers tremble as they worked at the delicate fastenings of the silk fabric, then at the front closure of the strapless bra. For a moment he did nothing at all, simply using his eyes to caress what he so badly wanted to touch. His gaze was so intense that she could almost feel the weight of it on her heated flesh. At last, when she thought she could wait no longer, his hand cupped her breast, capturing it.

Her warm, pulsating flesh filled his hand, the nipple hardening and teasing his palm. He bent his head to nuzzle the other breast, laving the circumference of smooth, creamy flesh before his mouth sought her hardened nipple. He kissed one breast, deserting it with regret as his mouth replaced his hand on the other.

Karen arched toward him, feeling a warm, moist heat between her legs, knowing that only his touch could satisfy her. She reached up to clasp the back of his neck, binding him to her even more tightly. At the same time, her other hand stole beneath the sweater, seeking out the warm, muscular hardness of his chest. His hips began to move over hers, the ridge of his arousal sending an electric shock deep within her body. She was warm inside, warm, waiting and ready to be filled. With him.

A sound galvanized him, a knock on the door. He felt Karen stiffen beneath him.

"Is there anything you need, David?" he heard Dorothy Sturgis's voice call through the door.

Only Karen, he groaned inwardly, desperately trying to regain some measure of control. Somehow he dredged up the strength to answer. "No. No, thank you."

Almost before David's words were out, Karen had torn herself from his embrace in an effort to put her clothes, if not her hair and makeup, into some semblance of order. "We—we can't," she choked out, shuddering at the aftershocks she felt from the electricity of his touch.

"I know," he said, his voice heavy with regret, his body one throbbing ache of frustration as he struggled to control his breathing.

Walking over to the chair, she picked up the crutches, handing them to him. When he looked at her blankly, she extended them to him once more. "You'll have to get up so I can open the sofa."

Balancing between the crutches had never seemed so difficult as when he watched her making up the bed for him. He wouldn't have felt any less shaky if there was nothing at all wrong with his legs, he admitted to himself wryly. The bed had two pillows. He would have given anything he possessed to be able to wake up the next morning with her head on the pillow next to his.

By the time she'd finished, David was able to breathe normally, even able to speak, though his voice was thicker than usual. "I'm sorry, Karen. I should have had more sense. All I can say is, it's been a long time since I've done any necking with a girl in her parents' house!"

"It may have been a long time, but I sure wouldn't say you're out of practice!" Karen laughed shakily. "I'll see you tomorrow."

"Can we leave right after breakfast?"

"I thought you were enjoying yourself here."

"I'd enjoy myself more if you and I were alone in my house."

"Yes. Well." She cleared her throat. "I think I might enjoy that, too."

11

DURING THE RIDE back to David's Worthington Valley home, Karen debated how and when she would tell him about her feelings for him. She finally decided to do so when they made love in his house for the first time. She tried to imagine what it would be like to have the freedom to express her desire for him in that most intimate of ways.

David said little during the ride from Annapolis. What could he say? *Drive faster? I hope your car breaks down so that you can't leave my house for a week—or longer? How about Silence is Golden, Carter*, he taunted himself. And said nothing.

Never had Karen felt so nervous coming to David's house, not even the night of the rainstorm. Then she'd come armed with an apology. Now she was armed with love. She got no farther than the entrance hall, because immediately on entering, he closed the front door, leaned against it for support and pulled Karen into his arms. She opened her mouth to say something. Whatever it was went unsaid as his hungry mouth captured her own, his tongue delving past her parted lips.

Her arms wound around him, clasping him to her body, wanting only to be as close to him as she could.

She heard him speak into her mouth. "Come with me." To his bedroom, he meant.

"Yes," she replied with no hesitation.

"I'd carry you if I could," he said, traces of regret in his voice as he leaned forward on his crutches.

"After all my mother's cooking, I'd be too heavy," she replied as she slid an arm around his lean waist.

Once in the bedroom, he said, "I want to undress you—to see you—touch you all over."

"On one condition."

"What is it?" he asked stiffly, mentally bracing himself.

"That I'm allowed to do the same to you."

"Yes," he breathed.

She allowed him to position her in the middle of the bed, on top of the comforter. His mouth sought hers in a deep, penetrating kiss as his hands sought to completely unveil what had only been partially revealed the night before. He slid his hands under her heathery wool sweater, and felt his pulse race as he discovered that there was nothing underneath but warm, quivering flesh.

David's hands whispered erotically over her sensitized flesh as he grasped the hem of the sweater and eased it up over her body. She had no time to feel the cool air on her skin. All she knew was the hypnotic touch of his long fingers as he outlined her slender throat and traced the delicate line of her collarbone.

Don't stop there, she begged silently, her head moving from side to side. Her breathing quickened, and her breasts arched upward, too, begging for his touch. Her relief was exquisite when his callused hands palmed her breasts. And it heightened almost unbearably when his warm lips and tongue laved first one hardening nipple, then the other. His hands skimmed down her sides to her slender waist, his fingers trembling at the closure of her slacks. Finally he tugged them down over her long legs, then trailed his fingers against her silk panties before removing them, too. "David," she moaned, arching toward him once more.

She watched through glazed eyes as he braced himself on his elbows, lowering his clothed body onto her naked one. Her tender breasts were caressed by the soft wool sweater she'd given him, her belly and legs pressing into his hard arousal through the strained fabric of his wool slacks. Unable to resist, she slid her hands under the sweater, her fingers molding and outlining the taut, rippling muscles of his back.

Suddenly he pulled away; he was no longer hovering over her. She felt bereft. "David?"

"Undress me, Karen. Touch me. Hold me. Please."

She nodded, moving to where he lay on his back, his blue eyes following her every move. "But before I do that . . ." She placed her hands at either side of his head and touched her mouth to his, parting his lips with her seeking tongue, returning the caress he'd given her.

"Yes, oh, yes," he gasped, his tongue delving into the sweet, moist cavern of her mouth. "I need you to touch me. I need to feel your hands on my body," he muttered almost feverishly.

She wanted to touch him so much, she realized as she removed the sweater, easing it up over his muscular torso, over his arms and very carefully over his face and head. Above all, she didn't want to hurt him. She placed her hands on his exposed rib cage while her mouth blazed a trail through the forest of hair on his chest, pausing to taste each masculine nipple.

"God, Karen. I—I can't stand it," he gasped, his hips grinding against her own naked ones.

Her trembling fingers fumbled at his belt, finally releasing it, her eyes widening at the tantalizing sight of his arousal through the taut material. Taking a deep breath, she eased down the zipper, unable to keep her hands away from his pulsating heat; it drew her like a magnet.

"Oh, God, lady, please hurry...!" David gasped, gently urging her to finish the job she'd started before he lost all control. Together they removed the rest of his clothes and dropped them to the floor, not caring where they landed. And then, very slowly and carefully, he positioned himself over her and took her in his arms. "You feel so good against me. I've wanted this for so damned long."

"So—have—I," she answered, punctuating her words with soft kisses.

He kissed her again while his hands learned the peaks and valleys, hollows and curves of her body. His hand found the golden triangle at the junction of her thighs, then the part of her that would come to know him soon. So soon.

He was a heavy weight on her body, a welcome weight. She nuzzled his throat, tasting the salt of his skin while her slender hand slid between their two bodies, her hand brushing his as it passed. She stroked the pulsating shaft of his arousal, feeling his breathing quicken, his body grow taut with unfulfilled desire.

"Karen, I need you. Now!"

"Yes, now. I need you, too."

The hot moistness inside her turned to liquid as she helped guide him into her velvety softness. At first he stayed sheathed within her. She was so tight....

When he didn't move, she looked up at him. His sweat-sheened face was tense with strain, the muscles of his arms rippling as he braced himself above her. "What's wrong?" she whispered, smoothing the hair back from his dampened forehead.

"Nothing—at all. You just feel . . . so good."

In response, her body began to arch toward him almost of its own accord, taking him deeper into the center of her being.

"Oh, sweet lady, you are so special," he gasped as he followed her lead, slowly at first, and then faster.

Caught unawares, Karen felt the light of a thousand candles explode within her as David brought her to the pinnacle of fulfillment—and beyond. At that moment, she was alone in the universe, poised over a precipice. And then, she wasn't alone anymore. He was with her, crying out his own release, falling with her toward the light.

When she opened her eyes, his were closed. She lay within the hard circle of his embrace, breast to chest, pelvis to pelvis, sharing everything, even the slick sheen of sweat. From her vantage point Karen could see his face, the furrowed scars still there, of course, but the bracketed lines of stress and tension somehow faded. She'd never seen him so relaxed. This she had done for him.

Wake up, David, she urged silently. *Wake up, so I can tell you something. I want to tell you now, when we're at our most vulnerable, when it's so very new, like a shiny copper penny. I want to give it to you, as my very special gift.* As if in answer to her silent plea, his eyes fluttered open, his gaze sleepy at first, but almost immediately fully alert as he claimed her mouth in a kiss of singular sweetness. But when he pulled back, opening his mouth as if to say something, Karen laid her fingers lightly across his lips, shaking her head. His eyes gleamed, but he made no move to dislodge her fingers.

"I love you, David," she told him softly.

She felt him stiffen then, to her amazement, saw the gleam fade from his sapphire-blue eyes, turning them into flat, cold stones. "What is it?" she whispered, sliding her fingers from his mouth.

He took a deep, ragged breath. "You—you said you loved me."

"Yes."

"Since when?"

She felt his withdrawal keenly. "Why the cross-examination?" Until then her naked flesh had felt the warmth of passion and desire. And love, she had fervently hoped. Now her skin was clammy, her arms covered with goose bumps. She pulled the edge of the heavy comforter around her for warmth. "Don't you believe me?"

"I'm sure you believe what you're saying, Karen. I—just don't happen to think it's true."

"You think I'm lying about this!" she cried, wondering how something so lovely could have turned into such a nightmare.

"No, I don't think you're lying. I think you're mistaken."

"Mistaken," she echoed scornfully.

"Yes."

"Do you think it was easy for me to let myself learn to love you? To think you could fill the emptiness inside me?"

"Have you—been with a man since your husband?" The hesitancy of his voice couldn't camouflage the cold intrusiveness of the question.

"No."

"All right. And then, there's proximity. You and I have been together for a while. It's natural—"

"The hell it is! It's not natural for me to go to bed with a colleague just because we work together!"

"I didn't say that. I realize you feel something for me—pity, compassion. I'm like Nick, the stray you picked up when it was abandoned."

"Nick at least reciprocates my feelings!"

"And I was probably a healthy challenge to your ego. Otherwise you wouldn't have fought so damned hard to get me to do this assignment."

"So, now you're saying I'll do anything for an assignment. Do you think I slept with Larson, too, you bastard?" she hissed as she flung back the comforter and scrabbled for her discarded clothes.

"Of course not! Karen, look at me."

"Not interested," she bit out as she concentrated on getting into her clothes as quickly as she could. She couldn't bear to feel his eyes on her naked flesh.

"You'll listen when I talk," he ordered, steel-strong fingers grasping her upper arm.

"All right. Say your piece and stop mauling me."

His fingers fell away from her as if he'd been burned. "Look, I'll say this just once, and that's it. I want you. I can't deny that—my body won't let me. But wanting isn't loving."

"You mean that anybody would do."

"No, anybody would *not* do! I want to make love to *you*."

"But you don't want to love me," she stated flatly.

The part of him that might have wanted to love her was like a limb that had atrophied. He knew what love had brought, from his parents in his growing-up years, and later, from Eleanor. Rejection. Betrayal. He wasn't about to take a chance and get involved, and lay himself open to the risk of being hurt again, not even for Karen.

"I—I can't love you. I don't think I can love anybody. I don't think I ever learned how," he murmured, as if he'd forgotten she was even in the room. "Remember what you wrote in that note to me? About darkness? Well, there's a darkness inside me, like a lead curtain. I can't see through it, and it's too heavy to lift."

"Only because that's the way you want it."

"I'm grateful to you," he went on as if she hadn't spoken.

"Keep your damned gratitude!"

"I can't do that. You got me back to the land of the living." Then, "I'm sorry I hurt you."

"You can keep that, too."

"Where are you going?" he demanded as he watched her hurriedly finish dressing.

"Home."

"Will you—be back?"

"Of course. You said it yourself. The assignment and the foreign correspondent who goes with it are a challenge to my ego!" she said in a voice that dripped acid. "By your calculations the other day, we—you—should finish up in about two weeks. I'll stick around for the duration, don't worry."

"You can still use the pool."

"No thanks. I think I'll go back to the Y."

"Do you—want a drink before you go?"

"No. I don't want anything."

David reached for his slacks, pulling them on, not bothering with sweater or shoes as he picked up the crutches and followed her from his bedroom.

Karen went to her purse, pulled out her key ring and removed David's key, handing it to him. "I wouldn't want to invade your privacy," she said with great dignity. And with that, walked out his front door.

David's fingers closed tightly over the key as he went to the window to watch her leave. He heard the familiar clatter of the Volvo's engine and the sound of the tires moving too fast on the gravel. But he didn't actually see Karen drive away. His eyes were too blurred with tears.

KAREN KEPT ON DRIVING until she was a mile from David's house. Then she pulled over to the side of the road, cut the engine and cried as she hadn't cried since Tim's death. Somewhere in her rational mind she was hearing things like, *this isn't really happening*, and *he didn't really mean that*. But, buckets of tears later, she began to realize the truth. To David, she was simply a cog in a machine. A piece of equipment. A way to get from one place to another. She wasn't a person. She was a thing to be used, this time as an outlet for his sexual frustration. And that made her feel somehow unclean.

The burgeoning love she'd felt for him began to shrivel. She hated him for despoiling the beautiful memory of their lovemaking. But more than that, she hated him for destroying the fantasies she had barely dared to entertain of what life might have been like, if she could have lived it with him.

12

KAREN DIDN'T STAY for a drink—not that night nor any of the succeeding nights that she worked with David. She did her job—nothing more, nothing less. When the assignment was nearly over, she told herself she felt only one thing—relief that she would soon be back at her old job and away from him.

Maybe in time she would be able to forget she'd ever met him. But one thing was certain: she would be even more careful in the future about getting involved. She didn't need any more pain; she didn't need any more men like him to sabotage her emotional equilibrium.

With the help of work she had been able to partially screen out the pain of Tim. But now, every time she picked up a camera, every time she put on her swimsuit at the Y—she could only think of David.

And as if that weren't enough, she developed the film in her camera and found the frame of David and Nick sitting by the Christmas tree. At first she was strongly tempted to consign the negative to the trash bin. But in the end she made a print from it, placing it on her coffee table next to the picture she'd taken on that darkened patio so many weeks before. And next to both of them was the copy of *Metro-Lights* Mickie had given her that day in September.

Now every time she walked into her living room, she would see a minigallery of David Carter photographs.

She decided she would keep them until the assignment was over. There was no possibility of keeping him out of her thoughts until then. And afterward she would take the photographs and destroy them, along with her memories of the man himself.

On New Year's Eve, which she spent with a glass of cheap red wine, she imagined David on the sofa beside her, gazing into an imaginary fireplace, sharing an imaginary bottle of Perrier-Jouet champagne. It was almost funny, she mused to herself, realizing, of course, that it wasn't funny at all. She'd managed to avoid involvement for so long, wanting to suffer no more hurt. And now look at her!

DAVID CARTER FOUND that his house was no longer the haven it had been. Everything in it reminded him of Karen. The living room—they'd worked there constantly. It had a fireplace that reminded him of the one at her parents' house, and of how they'd almost made love there. The kitchen held memories of shared meals. And the lap pool now seemed too big for one person.

When he lay down on the king-size bed at night, he could almost feel the ghostly touch of her fingers as they'd given him comfort. And his body—and mind—ached as he remembered too well what it had felt like when, only a short time ago, she had given him her passion, and given him her love.

He hardly saw Karen anymore; she'd taken to using the courier whenever she could. He missed her feistiness, the smell of her perfume, even the disreputable cap she always wore on a job. He wished he could have told himself that he didn't care.

He wasn't capable of a lie of such magnitude, even to himself.

THE LAST INTERVIEW was to be in two stages, split between a Friday and a Monday. Karen needed photographs only from the first session, so she felt a weight lift from her shoulders when she headed the car back into the city on Friday afternoon. One more day of chauffeuring and the assignment really *was* over. Also over would be her involvement in David's life and his involvement, however slight it was now, in hers.

When she got back to the paper on Friday, it was nearly six o'clock and dark outside. She hurried, the collar of her down jacket turned up against the bitter-cold wind. Once inside the blessedly warm building, she went directly to the darkroom on the fourth floor. When she found *Met* photo technician Gary Jordan there, she asked him how soon she could get her film developed.

"Are you on deadline?"

She sighed, wishing she could lie. "Not for the paper, no." And at his puzzled expression, she went on to say with as little emotion as possible, "These are the last images from an assignment I've been working on since last September with David Carter. My esteemed colleague wants me to bring them out to his place tomorrow morning, so he can have them to look at this weekend. He likes to think of text and photographs as one unit. And I was hoping to do a lot of nothing this weekend."

Gary was shaking his blond head regretfully. "I really wish I could, but the enlarger's on the fritz, and the dryer is having its problems."

"What are you doing about tomorrow morning's edition and the Sunday paper?"

"Everything's being sent out for processing."

"Can my stuff go along with it?"

"It could have, if you hadn't just missed the courier," he said apologetically. "The next batch of film won't be back until tomorrow, if you want to wait that long."

No, she decided instantly. Better to get it over with once and for all. "I'll develop them at home and bring the negatives and everything back with me. Maybe I should rent out my darkroom to the *Met*," Karen said with a laugh as she waved goodbye to Gary.

Gadget bag on her shoulder, hands gloveless because she'd left her ski mittens in the car, she took the stairs, not bothering to wait for the elevator. She made her way out of the building, intending to go across the street to the underpass where she'd parked the Volvo. She never reached it. Before she'd even rounded the corner of the building, an arm snaked out, grabbing her by the shoulder, then slamming her against the brick wall, where she slid to the cold ground.

"The money—now," a rough voice growled in her ear.

"I—I don't have much, not even my purse," she managed, wishing with all her might for a policeman—a passerby—anyone.

"Then I'll just take this." He pulled at the strap of the heavy camera bag on her shoulder.

"No! You can't!"

She felt an explosion of pain as his fist struck her cheek. Then, in the dimness, she saw a glint of metal. She put a hand up to protect her face, felt a burning pain. And then . . . nothing.

THE NEXT THING SHE KNEW, someone was calling her name. She tried to answer, but she couldn't seem to get the words out.

"Don't worry, Ms Anderson," the voice said in calming tones. "I radioed back to the building, and they're calling for an ambulance."

Forever after Karen would wonder what had happened to her and why—whether it was because she was too preoccupied and too careless, or whether it was simply one of life's inevitable cruelties. What followed was a maze of pain, confusion and fear that such a thing could happen to her right outside the building where she worked, almost in plain view. If someone hadn't come along . . . She shuddered at the thought.

"Cold?"

She tried to look in the direction of the voice.

"No, don't try to move, Ms Anderson. I'm Dr. Riley. You're at Mercy Hospital. You have bruised ribs, the beginnings of a black eye and some stitches in your right hand."

"Other than that I'm fine?" she queried in a shaky whisper.

"Glad to see you haven't lost your sense of humor."

"No, just my cameras. I—I don't suppose the man was caught?"

"Sorry. Do you feel well enough to talk to the police?"

"Yes."

Two uniformed officers came in and took her statement. But they held out no encouragement that her cameras would ever be found. She was lucky that her keys and identification had been in her pocket, she was told. Otherwise the man might be turning up on her

doorstep. *A reassuring thought*, she groaned inwardly, realizing that she'd joined the ranks of victims
of urban crime. She was now a statistic, one of the
number that contradicted all assurances to the public
that "Crime is going down." If the policemen found out
anything about the cameras, they would let her know.
She thanked them for their efforts, then turned her attention back to the doctor who had entered on their
heels. "When can I leave?" she asked him.

"We want to keep you for at least twenty-four hours,
because you were unconscious for a short time."

"Not for very long."

"It doesn't take very long for a head injury to take a
turn for the worse, unless you've got someone at home
who can take care of you."

She wasn't about to call her parents and worry them.
And as far as she was concerned, there was no one else,
which is what she told the doctor.

"No one from the paper?"

She thought of Mickie, but the librarian lived all the
way up near the Maryland-Pennsylvania border and
would have left for home long since. "No," she said
firmly, "there's no one I'd want to impose on."

Once she was assigned to a semi-private room, she
called Don Ross, who offered to come and get her.
Warmed by his response, she told him she was perfectly satisfied to stay where she was. It wasn't absolutely true, but then being mugged was rather
hazardous to one's health, she decided.

In the end she stayed in the hospital Friday night, all
day Saturday and left on Sunday morning, assured that
she had no lasting injuries and that the shiner would

disappear. The stitches on her hand could come out in a week; she should keep the wound dry until then.

She took a cab home from the hospital, because the doctor didn't want her driving until the swelling on her eye had receded. Also, the bandage on her right hand would have made handling the Volvo's temperamental stick shift awkward. Once she'd settled in, she called Don to tell him she was back home.

"Don't come back until you're ready," he insisted. "And let me know how you're doing. Oh, and we'll take care of your car."

"Will you tell David? I mean, since I was assigned..."

"I'll take care of it. You just take it easy. Call the insurance company about the cameras as soon as you can. In the meantime, I have a couple of spares you can use if they're slow in coming across with the cash. Turn down the ringer on your phone so you don't get anybody disturbing your rest. Feel better, Karen."

She had felt somewhat better—until she looked in the mirror and saw the myriad colors and swellings that were now her face. She ate lightly, then took one of the painkillers the doctor had prescribed. The pain lessened, but her sleep was restless and filled with nightmares. When the pain started up again on Monday morning, she shoved the pills back into the closet, deciding that physical pain was easier to handle than the mental anguish the nightmares brought.

WHEN KAREN DIDN'T SHOW UP on Saturday morning, David called her home, but got no answer. He called again on Sunday, and still there was no answer. Granted, things hadn't exactly been cordial between them since that day after Christmas, but he was beginning to get annoyed. She'd promised him the films by Saturday morning, dammit! Maybe she'd been too busy to bother. A knife turned deep inside his guts at the thought of her with another man. He told himself it was none of his business who she was involved with.

But by Monday afternoon, when she didn't show up to drive him to a three o'clock interview, his temper went through the roof. He called her at home; still no answer. So he called the photography department at the paper to speak to Don Ross.

"Where the hell is Karen this afternoon?" David demanded. "And where are my films? She was supposed to have them for me on Saturday morning. And she never showed up or even called. She didn't come in today, either. I had to cancel an interview."

"Now isn't that too damned bad?" Ross replied.

"Now look here—"

"No, you look. And shut the hell up so I can get a word in edgewise. We've been buried under a ton of breaking news this weekend, and I'm a photographer short, so I've had a damned sight more to worry about than your interview schedule. Calling you wasn't exactly tops on my list of priorities. Now about Karen— she's out sick, because she was mugged on Friday night."

"Mugged?" David's hand tightened on the phone, his every nerve pervaded by the icy touch of cold fear.

"Second," Ross continued, ignoring the other man's interruption, "I told her to take some time off. Now if you want another photographer to retake those shots, you tell me."

"No," he muttered hoarsely, more to himself than to the man on the other end of the line. "No, I'll wait for her. You say she's home? There's no answer when I called."

"I told her to lay low, get some rest and ignore the phone. Don't hassle her, Carter."

"I won't, don't worry."

Hassle her! He only wanted to see her. He called a cab, giving the driver Karen's Federal Hill address. It was nearly five o'clock. He wouldn't get to her house until nearly six, he thought, wishing there was some way he could get there faster.

"Vietnam?" the driver asked as the cab crossed the city line.

"What?"

"Were you shot up in 'Nam?"

"The Middle East."

"Rough."

"Yeah."

The cab pulled up on Churchill Street at five minutes before six.

"You need any help with those steps? My brother lost a leg in 'Nam. He says steps are a bitch."

David glanced at the four steps in front of Karen's apartment. "I'll be fine. Thanks for asking."

He made it up the four stone steps to the front door, but a lock with a remote switch barred him from going any farther. He shivered in the cold as he took a deep breath, then pressed the button marked Anderson—2-A.

When Karen heard the buzzing of the front door, she wanted nothing more than to ignore it, hoping it would go away. When it became obvious that was never going to happen, she went to the intercom. "Who is it?"

"David."

She had to hang on to the doorjamb to combat the sudden weakness in her knees. "David who?"

"David Carter! Who do you think?" he grated.

"Go away."

That he hadn't expected. "Karen, it's a very long twenty miles from where I live to where you live."

"You should have thought of that before you came down here uninvited. What do you want?"

"To see you."

"I don't want to see you."

That was beginning to appear rather obvious. "Will you at least let me come up so I can call a cab?"

"A cab?"

"How do you think I got here?"

She barely refrained from telling him she couldn't care less. "I'll call one for you. You don't have to come up."

"There's no telling when a cab will come. It's damned cold out here, and there's no place to sit." There was a long silence before he heard a resigned, "All right. Come up. I'll leave the door unlocked for you."

David heard the sound of a buzzer, then pushed open the heavy glass door to the second floor. He counted eleven steps between the first- and second-floor landing. Eleven steps, all hard and wooden. "Mount Everest, I presume," he muttered determinedly as he gritted his teeth and began climbing, one step at a time. It took him nearly ten minutes of sweat and hard work to make it to the top of those stairs. When he reached the landing, he headed for the doorway, anchoring the crutches as if he were planting a flag at the summit. Then he just stood there, heart pounding, muscles cramping, breathless from his effort. He could hardly wait to figure out a way to get down.

"Karen?" he called as he opened the door.

"In the bedroom."

He started for it, barely noticing the furnishings in the room as he made his way to her bedroom door.

She heard him coming through the living room and knew instinctively where he was headed—straight for her. "Stay where you are!"

"Do you need any help?" he asked, his chest heaving as he gratefully took advantage of the burgundy-velvet sofa, leaning against it for support. "Is there anything I can do for you?"

"No. You're only here on sufferance, long enough for you to pick up that phone and call a cab. I suggest you do it!"

The hell he would! He hadn't hiked all the way up here only to go back home without accomplishing his goal. And since she refused to come out, he would have to go in to see her. Her voice had sounded muffled. Lord, maybe she was hurt worse than Ross had told him. Maybe Ross didn't even know; he hadn't gone to see her, after all. Ignoring the fatigue that threatened to swamp him, he headed once more for her bedroom, determined to make as little noise as possible.

She was lying on her side, facing away from the door, curled up into herself, under a comforter. Her shoulders heaved as if she were fighting for control. Every once in a while there was a noise that sounded suspiciously like a cross between a sigh and a sob. He edged closer to the bed.

"Why did you come?" she asked him resignedly, not looking up at him.

"Why do you think I came?"

"You wanted that latest set of films. Well, they were in the cameras that he—he took from me. I'll have to reshoot them. Or you can get somebody else, I guess. What did you do about the interview today?"

"I canceled it."

"When I didn't show up."

"Yeah."

"I'm sorry."

Sorry? She was sorry, when he was the fool who should be apologizing? Damn. Slowly, carefully, he sat down on the edge of the bed, removing the crutches and leaning them against the night table. With his left hand braced on the headboard for support, he laid his right hand gently, very gently on the shoulder nearest to him. When she shrank from his touch, he removed his hand immediately, resting both hands, palms down, on the bed just beside her. "I wanted to see how you were."

"You could have called."

"I did. I didn't get any answer. Did you expect me to write a note?"

"I didn't expect anything."

That hurt. "Karen."

"Did you call a cab?"

"No."

"Call one."

"No. Not until I see you."

"Don't hold your breath."

"What are you afraid of? You're not afraid—of me?" he asked, inwardly fearing her answer.

As much as he'd hurt her, as great as the pain had been, and still was, she knew she couldn't lie. Not about that. "N-no," was her wobbly response.

He breathed a sigh of relief. "Then why won't you look at me?" he asked gently. "You've never hesitated before."

"I never had a reason to before."

"You don't have a reason now," he countered.

"You'll—laugh at me."

"Laugh? I can't think of anything even remotely funny about any of this."

It was crystal clear to Karen that David wasn't going to leave until he got what he came for, which was evidently a sight of his soon-to-be former colleague in all her black-and-blue-and-green glory. *So be it*, she thought wearily, moving her hair to one side.

As she slowly turned toward him, his breath hissed out in shock. Her right eye was black-and-blue, the skin around it and her jaw multicolored and scraped in places. "God!" He felt a surge of raw, pure anger at the man—no, the animal—who had done this to her. Without stopping to think, he edged closer to her, drawing her satin-covered softness gently into his arms and against his chest, being careful not to touch the injured side of her face. He felt her stiffen, then try to pull away as he began to stroke her hair.

"All right!" she grated, her voice muffled against the soft wool of his sweater. "You've seen what you came to see. You've satisfied your curiosity. Now you can leave. Let go of me and get out! I don't want you here." It was hard enough knowing David didn't love her. Having him here in her bedroom, actually touching her, brought agony even more painful than the mugging.

Those bruises would fade. The scars David had gouged in her heart would not.

He winced at the hardness in her voice as he laid her back against the pillows. His heart quickened, threatening to suffocate him as he saw the V of her peach-colored satin nightgown part over the creamy curves of her breasts. Striving for control, he pulled the comforter up to her shoulders. His eyes narrowed as he saw the bandage on her right hand. "What happened to your hand?" he asked quietly.

"It's a...souvenir of my little adventure, I guess you could say."

"I see." He assumed she must have bruised or sprained it falling to the ground. "Have you eaten today?"

She shrugged, relieved that he was finally finished taking inventory of her injuries.

"I'll fix you something."

"No, thanks. I'm not hungry."

He got to his feet so quickly that he almost overbalanced, and had to hang on to the headboard for support. "You're always hungry. It's one of your charms," he replied as he went off in the direction of the kitchen.

She was determined not to move. He wouldn't be able to carry the food in all by himself. He would get tired of her unwillingness to yield to him. And he would leave. He would have to. Then she could be alone again, so that she could start the process of learning how to forget him.

David was perfectly at home in his own kitchen; Karen's was little different. Even though he was half-exhausted, it didn't take him very long to locate the makings for a simple but nourishing meal. Fast. He could rest after she'd eaten, he told himself as he gathered everything together. Of course, it would have been easier if she'd agreed to eat in the kitchen. But he could hardly force her to do that. So then the problem became how to get the tray to her. He knew damned well that he couldn't carry it; physical therapy hadn't taken him that far. Yet. Glancing around the small, comfortable country kitchen, he searched for a solution and found one sitting in front of a window, camouflaged by a number of potted plants. . . .

Karen closed her eyes, willing David to disappear, listening for the sound of the front door closing. The next thing she knew, there was an odd series of sounds—squeaking, scraping, rolling, and a muffled curse or two for punctuation. "What!" Unbelievably, David, using only one crutch, was pushing her plantless plant cart into the bedroom. "What—in—the—world?"

"The mountain came to Mohammed," he told her, a grin half lifting the side of his mouth and masking just how much effort it had taken him to push that mountain across the carpeted floors of Karen's apartment. Still, he'd made it with only one crutch and no serious mishaps. Maybe he'd be graduating to a cane even sooner than he'd hoped.

Karen watched his slow progress as he pushed the table to her bedside. She struggled to sit up, but he was there beside her, pulling her toward him as he mounded the pillows behind her back for support. He sat down next to her then, glad to be off his feet, if truth were told. He pushed the cart right up to the edge of the bed so both he and Karen had access to it.

She reached for the plate with her left hand, more than a little annoyed when David shook his head. "I thought you wanted me to eat?"

"I do, but I thought you were right-handed?"

"I am."

"So I'm going to make it easier on you." He cut into the egg, then raised the fork until it was poised at her mouth.

She blushed furiously, shaking her head. She wasn't about to let him feed her!

"Are you hungry, Karen?"

"Yes!"

"Then open your mouth," he ordered softly.

In the end, she allowed him to feed her the eggs, interspersed with bites of marmalade toast. He very graciously allowed her to use her left hand to drink her coffee. He was looking so smug and self-satisfied with his efforts that Karen snapped, "Okay. You've done your good deed for the day. You've fed the starving invalid. Now I'm going to sleep. Goodbye, David."

He shook his head solemnly. "I'll get these out of your way," he said, nodding toward the dishes. "Then you can go to sleep."

"Leave the dishes, I don't care. Just—go!"

"I would if I could," he said wistfully.

She stared at him. "What does that mean?"

"I can't."

"You can't what?"

"Leave."

"Why not?"

"Two reasons, the first being that I don't want you to be alone here."

"I don't need a baby-sitter."

He had certainly never thought of Karen as a child. "You don't want to stay here alone, do you?"

"I live alone," she reminded him.

"Does anyone live downstairs?"

"It's not rented."

"You could stay with your parents."

"I'm not about to call them. They'd only worry. I'm not exactly at death's door, you know. And don't get any ideas about calling them, either."

"I might just have to." There was an evil gleam in his eyes.

"You will not!"

"At Christmas, your mother said she was glad there was somebody to look after you in the city," he reminded her.

"Give me a break!"

"That's what I'm trying to do. You shouldn't be alone."

"You managed alone all that time in your house out in the Valley."

"Yes, I did. But that doesn't mean it was right." He grimaced at Karen's barely concealed gasp of shock at what he'd just said. "And it's certainly not right for you."

"What gives you the right to tell me what to do?"

"The right of a—a colleague. We're that, certainly."

"Don Ross is a colleague, and he's not telling me what to do."

"We used to be friends, you and I. Isn't that right?"

"Not—close friends." *Just lovers for a single, solitary, lovely moment in time*, she recalled with bittersweet melancholy.

"No," he conceded.

And whose fault is that, she thought bleakly. "I want you to go away. Now. I don't care about being here alone, or your opinions about it, either. I just want you gone!" *Oh, God,* she cried silently, *I can't stand this. It's bad enough working with him. Having him right here next to me and knowing I mean nothing to him....*

When it became abundantly clear that he had no intention of leaving, she asked in a tired voice, "What's your other reason for not leaving?"

He took a deep breath as a flush crept across his face. "I'm ... not used to stairs. I can't get down them again, not today, anyway." That wasn't perfectly true, he acknowledged to himself. He could have made it back down the stairs. It simply would have hurt like hell, and meant that he'd be even more stiff and sore than he was already. Admitting weakness went against the grain, and against his pride. But getting her to allow him to stay with her far outweighed that. "Climbing those eleven stairs took a lot out of me," he said truthfully, giving his ego yet another body blow.

"Oh, David," she whispered helplessly, seeing all at once how gray and tired he looked. And remembering how, for the first time since the afternoon of the Wyatt interview, his gait had seemed awkward and unsteady as he walked.

"I'm not playing on your sympathies, you know," he said, even though he knew he was.

"No, of course not. I'm sorry you went to all this trouble."

"Don't be any more stupid than you can help, Karen. I know you didn't ask me to come." He wished she had. Taking a deep breath, he said, "What's the matter with my staying here?"

"I can't believe you have the gall to ask!"

"You might need something."

"I'll manage. Why should you worry about whether or not I need something?"

Because I care. But there was no way he was going to tell her that. Given her state of mind, there was no way she was going to believe him. And why should she, after all? "You'll just have to put up with me until I can get down the stairs again."

She had to bite her lip to keep from asking sarcastically when that would be. "Suit yourself."

AFTER CLEARING AWAY the remnants of Karen's dinner, David fixed eggs for himself. Then he asked his reluctant hostess for a sheet for the sofa. She gave him that, along with a pillow and an afghan, then lay down on her own bed, wondering how he was managing in the other room. The couch really wasn't long enough for him, was it? But he'd brought the discomfort on himself.

Karen tried desperately to sleep. Was it possible that everything ached worse today than it had on Friday night after the attack? She hardly knew which way to turn. Exhaustion weighted her eyelids, but it was the pain pill she'd taken that hastened her fall into a restless sleep....

I sure didn't come prepared to stay overnight, David thought wryly as he slipped off the sweater and slacks, leaving them on the back of an upholstered rocking chair. He wondered if Karen would mind his sleeping in his undershirt and briefs. She probably would never know, he decided as he lay down on the sofa and covered himself with the afghan.

He certainly hadn't lied to Karen, he told himself later
as he tried to get comfortable on a sofa not designed for
sleeping a man of his height. The muscles in his legs and
thighs ached viciously from his efforts on the stairs. In
spite of all the strengthening exercises that were a part
of his therapy routine, stairs were beyond his abilities.
He didn't care, though. He wasn't in her apartment for
R and R, but to *be* there—just in case. He shifted the
pillow once more behind his head, then lay back and
closed his eyes.

When sleep didn't come, he opened his eyes and
looked at the array of framed and loose photographs
on the glass-topped coffee table, images that he'd just
barely glanced at when entering the apartment. The
photographs didn't surprise him. They were her business, after all. Without any thought of prying, he
picked up the one closest to hand, and saw that it was
a color photograph of a laughing man flying a kite. Or
trying to fly one. She'd certainly managed to catch the
spirit of the moment on film, he marveled. And suddenly he knew without a doubt that the man in the
photograph was her late husband, Tim. Very gently he
set the framed image back where he'd found it.

The other pictures were a decided shock to his system, however. Also in a frame was the first image Karen
had taken in the garden on that memorable night in the
fall. The second was the one she'd taken at Christmas,
with Nick the dog at his feet. And the third was a back
copy of *Metro-Lights*, including a photograph taken
just after his arrival in the Middle East.

For a moment all he felt was shock—but not at seeing
the man who looked as if he didn't have a care in the
world. The face in the image wasn't really so different

from the one he saw in the mirror every morning. Except for a few additions. What shocked him was the fact that Karen had seen the picture. But then, why should it bother him that she'd seen the old David Carter, the man he'd once been?

She hadn't turned away from what he looked like on the outside, after all. She had rejected what she'd found on the inside, and even then only after he'd caused her pain. What had she written in that note all those months before? Oh, yes: maybe people turned away from the emptiness that looked out from his eyes.

He returned the *Met*'s in-house tabloid to the table and lay back on the sofa once again. Lacing his hands behind his head, he focused all his mental efforts on trying not to imagine his future without Karen.

13

AT FIRST he didn't know what had awakened him. Then his senses came fully alert as he heard moans, soft at first, then rising on a crescendo of pain. "Karen!" He reached out for the crutches, almost toppling the coffee table, cursing as he struggled to get to her bedroom as fast as he could.

She was tossing and turning, crying, her head moving from one side of the pillow to the other. The sight of her bruised face glistening with tears tore at his heart. "Karen," he called softly as he eased himself onto the bed next to her. There was no response. One of her flailing arms struck his shoulder. He grasped her hand before she could hurt herself.

"No!" she cried, physical pain tearing through the coils of nightmare. "Don't hurt me!"

Immediately his fingers went lax. "I'd never hurt you, Karen."

"You already have," she whispered, turning her face away from the familiar voice just at the edge of her dream.

"Wake up," he urged, ignoring the pain her words had caused him. "You're having a nightmare." Unable to bear her suffering, he leaned over, drawing her into his arms. "It's all right," he crooned into her ear. His hand smoothed damp hair back from her forehead and away from the back of her neck. His fingers ranged over her nape, rhythmically kneading until her shaking sobs began to subside.

It felt so good—so right—to be in his arms, her head in the hollow of his shoulder. But it had felt right before, and all she'd been left with was heartache. She forced herself to remain passive, wanting to stay there always but knowing she couldn't. She could feel his heartbeat surging against her as her breasts grazed the soft cotton undershirt covering his muscular chest. For an instant his hold tightened, almost crushing her to him. Then she felt him lower her to the pillows, settling her under the covers, almost as if she were a beloved child.

"Do you want to talk about it, what happened to you Friday night?"

"No. You can go back to sleep," she told him dismissively. "I'm all right."

"You don't look it."

So don't look, she wanted to say. "Thanks."

"Talking things out might help."

"How do you know?"

"Experience." He knew what it was like not to have anyone to tell his troubles to. Too well. There had been no one to listen, until Karen had eased her way into his life. "Talk to me, honey."

Somehow the softly spoken endearment reached her. "It wasn't anything unusual, really. They don't even write it up for the paper anymore. It happens too often. I was just leaving the building. I had my gadget bag on my shoulder. The man decided he wanted it, and we struggled."

"Why didn't you just give him the damned cameras?" he demanded harshly.

"Those cameras are my life. Besides, I had the films I'd promised you in there."

"Oh, my God!" he groaned.

"Yes, well, the man got what he wanted."

"That's the short version," he stated bluntly.

"Persistent, aren't you?"

"Nothing but. I'm an investigative reporter, Karen. Do I have to dig up a police report to find out what happened to you?"

She took a deep breath and had to swallow before she could go on. "He—hit me, slammed me into the brick wall of the *Met*, and I slid to the ground. But the worst thing was that he . . . had a knife," she concluded brokenly, her voice trailing off into a whisper as she saw in her mind's eye the glint of the blade.

For a moment David felt his heart jolt to a stop as he sat frozen in fear. "A knife? He came at you with a knife?"

"Yes. No. It wasn't like that. He meant to cut the strap on the bag, I guess. I—I thought he was going for my face, so I put up my hand, and that's how it happened. It isn't bad, honestly. Just a few stitches that come out next week."

He picked up her right hand, cradling it between his own, which were none too steady. He bent his head so that he could press his lips to her fingers just below the place where the bandage came to an end. "Do you have much pain?" he asked, his voice muffled.

"Some," she admitted, mesmerized by the sight of him bending to kiss her hand and by the feel of his warm mouth on her aching flesh.

"Did they give you any pills?"

"I took one before. I think that's why I had the nightmare. I couldn't wake up."

"It won't happen again."

"How can you say that?"

"Because I won't let it.

"What does that mean?"

"It means that I'm staying right here beside you tonight. No protests or arguments allowed. If you start to have a nightmare, I'll wake you." When she looked down, shaking her head, he placed his free hand very gently under her chin so that she was looking up at him. "You trusted me to keep the nightmares at bay once before. Do you remember?"

How could she forget the time she'd massaged away his headache—and discovered her love for him. "I remember," she whispered, her jaw brushing his fingers.

"Will you trust me to do it once more?" he asked, holding his breath as he waited for her answer.

She nodded, then backed away from his touch.

The movement, clearly a rejection, tore at his insides, but he only said quietly, "I'll get you that pill."

"I can get it," she said, edging off the bed, telling herself that the less contact she had with him, the better off she'd be. "I have to go to the bathroom," she informed him gently when he protested.

He watched her walk out of the room, gritting his teeth at her unaccustomed slowness and the way she occasionally paused to use the wall for support. His fists clenched as his mind pictured what had happened to her. For the first time in his life he felt an almost primitive need to do violence—to the slimy lowlife who'd laid hands on her. Then he heard the footsteps that told him of her return to the bedroom. Deliberately he forced himself to relax, knowing Karen needed his strength, not his unexploded rage.

As she neared the doorway, he edged toward the far side of the mattress and lay flat on his back, trying to stem his awareness of the woman who would lie so close to him, yet so far away. He wanted her but he knew he could never have her. She didn't want him. Not now. But for tonight at least, for these moments out of time, she would accept his comfort.

When she came back from the bathroom, she saw that he'd stretched out on the far side of the bed. She lay down at the opposite edge of the mattress, her back to him.

David watched her and saw that she barely moved, even to breathe. "Relax. Let the pill do its work. I won't touch you. I'll just be here if you need me." At first he was certain she was going to ignore him. But then she shifted sightly, obviously seeking a more comfortable position.

He tried hard to stay awake, his senses constantly on the alert for signs of distress from Karen's side of the bed. But eventually tiredness won out, and he drifted off to sleep just as the sounds of the waking city began coming to life outside the window. Sometime in those early hours of the morning, she must have turned toward him, because when he awoke, her slender warmth was nestled into the hardness of his body. Her head lay in the hollow of his shoulder, her bandaged right hand on his chest, just beneath his breastbone.

The comforter had shifted toward the lower half of the bed, and her hair, shining in the brightness of the sun, draped his bare arm in tangled silk. At first he didn't move a muscle, wanting only to savor her closeness for as long as he could. Then he felt her stir. Fearing she was cold, he extended his free hand, pulling the comforter up over both of them.

Karen awoke to find herself cloaked in David's embrace. His arms held her close to him; one of his legs was thrown over her slender thighs in an almost protective attitude. The uninjured side of her face was cradled against the hardness of his chest. And the solid, rhythmic drumming of his heartbeat in her ear set up an answering clamor in her own breast. The voice of reason told her it was time to get up and away from him. Another voice—one she tried to ignore—advised her to stay where she was until the last possible moment. The voice of reason won.

"David." His name on her lips was a husky whisper.

"Hmm?"

"Let me up."

"Sorry," he said, regretfully easing away from her, then leaning on his side facing her, propping himself up on his elbow. "Shall I fix you breakfast?"

"No time."

"What's your hurry?"

"I've got to take a bath, then get dressed."

"I'll help you with that bath so you don't get your hand wet."

"Never mind." She sighed. No way was she going to relearn the touch of his hands on her body. "I'll skip the bath and get dressed."

"Going somewhere?" he asked idly, watching her from his relaxed position as she rummaged about in drawers.

"Work," she replied, her voice muffled as she delved into a closet.

"The hell you are!" he growled, sitting straight up in bed. "Where did you get that crazy idea?"

"I'm going down to the paper to borrow a couple of cameras from Don."

"Do you mean to tell me he had the gall to hand you an assignment when you can't even see out of both eyes?"

"I'm a professional. I'm going to reshoot what I took the day I was mugged."

"No way, lady."

"You don't have any right to tell me what to do."

"The films don't matter."

"How can you say that?"

"Forget the damned films. Films aren't important— hell, nothing's important when someone you love is hurt. You mean more to me than a whole gallery of pictures!" His heart raced with shock at what he'd just blurted out.

"But it would have finished the assignment and—" She broke off in midsentence, staring at him, the salt of tears burning her eyes. "What—did—you—say?"

"I love you," he stated flatly.

"I don't believe you," she countered, the stark words motivated by the pain and hurt she'd received from him that awful day after Christmas. "Why tell me this now?"

"Because it's true!"

"Oh, come on," she scoffed. "When did this happen? In the last twenty minutes? When you saw the bruises? Or when you first heard I'd been mugged?"

He felt intense pain, as well as a shattering sense of anticlimax. *Give it up, Carter. You blew it. She'll never believe you. And why should she, after all? You did*

such a good job convincing her that you didn't love her.
But he couldn't give it up. It was too important, even if
it meant sacrificing his pride. "Before that. Way before
that. I—"

"You feel sorry for me," she cut in before he could
continue. "You feel compassion. Pity. Just what you
told me I felt for you."

"They're real feelings. Why shouldn't I feel sorry for
your pain?"

"That isn't love."

"No. But this is." His body invaded her territory, his
lips capturing hers, his tongue seeking entrance to her
mouth, his hand urgently caressing the soft peak of her
breast through the satin gown.

She fought to subdue her feelings, determined to respond with icy coldness, to tell him without words that
his actions were too little, too late—that they meant
nothing. But her body turned traitor as her breathing
quickened, her taut nipple sought the palm of his hand,
her mouth yielded to the invasion of his tongue. When
finally he eased away from her, she was filled with self-
disgust, both at her own behavior and at the triumph
she read in his blue eyes.

"You can't deny that you feel something for me,
Karen—that we mean something to each other."

"And you want to call it 'love.' Well, as you told me
that very memorable day in your house, I can't deny
that my body wants you. But that doesn't mean I won't
deny my body."

"You've got a photographic memory, haven't you?
You remember everything I say. I did my work too well,
didn't I?" There was a bitter edge to his voice. "Well,
dammit, you were so ready to believe my elaborate lies,

why can't you believe the simple truth when you hear it?" he growled, turning away from her.

Something—the note of despair in his voice—penetrated the depth of the icy barrier that Karen had erected. She turned toward him, calling his name softly. When he didn't respond, she tugged gently at his shoulder, and felt the tremors that shook him. Gradually she felt him turn, yielding slowly to her insistent touch.

To her horror, she saw that his eyes were filled with tears. "Oh, David—don't." She saw his throat work convulsively as he swallowed twice.

"Sorry," he managed. "I'm—sorry." One hand attempted to stem the moisture in his eyes.

"What is the truth? Tell me. If you love me, then why did you reject me after Christmas? Why did you do that to me?"

"Watching you walk out the door that day was the hardest thing I've ever done, believe me. But I knew it wouldn't be fair to you. I hadn't come to terms with myself. I couldn't come to terms with loving you, either. I was afraid to get involved, afraid to trust my love for you, to count on the love you said you felt for me.

"But even more than that, I didn't know if I could be the right person for you, someone to fill the emptiness, not pull you down into some black hole. You need someone loving and kind—"

"What makes you think you're not that person? I do," she said as she placed a tender kiss at the corner of his mouth.

He shook his head, very nearly coming apart inside at the effort it cost him not to respond to her. He wanted so badly to accept what she was offering but he knew he could never live with himself if the words went unsaid.

"Experience is the best teacher," he muttered, his voice so low she had to strain to hear him. "I haven't done too well at love in the past. Promises of love have always been withheld, or if given, have been withdrawn or disintegrated. That's the kind of baggage I bring with me to a relationship. Not a terrific track record," he concluded with a shrug.

She said nothing, knowing he was thinking of his parents and of the woman he'd almost married.

"And then there was that time on Sugar Loaf Mountain," he added, the bitterness of memory eating away at his guts. "God! I felt so helpless, so inadequate. I couldn't take care of you."

"You managed though, even then. And you're here now, aren't you, David? You came, even though I didn't call you."

"That hurt, Karen—that you didn't call me."

"I didn't think I had the right to do that," she said softly, telling him the bitter truth.

"I'd have walked, if I'd had to."

"And you stayed, even though I didn't want you here. Is there more to this—this truth of yours?"

He took a deep breath. "I wanted you to be happy."

"Really! Do I look happy to you? For two years after Tim I avoided getting involved with anyone. At first I was afraid of being disloyal to his memory. Then I told myself there was no one I could care about. But deep down I think I always knew I was afraid of going through that awful agony of losing someone I loved. I didn't want to go through it again. And then you had to come along."

"And I hurt you, Karen. I never will again, I swear it. I've loved you ever since the moment you looked at me and didn't flinch. I want to spend the rest of my life proving it to you, if you'll let me. But, my God, you're so beautiful."

"Even now, black eye and all?"

"Especially now. And you deserve...somebody whole, Karen."

"You are whole, David. And you're beautiful, too," she said. And without stopping to think, Karen kneeled beside him, laying her bandaged hand lightly on his shoulder.

"Have you looked in my mirror lately?" he asked drily.

"You don't need a mirror," she told him. Her hands clasped either side of his head, her fingers entwined in the darkness of his hair, anchoring him so that he couldn't move, couldn't look away. "Now I have you where I want you, Mr. Carter. And you're going to listen to what I have to say! I love you. Believe it! Look into my eyes."

He tilted his head and saw twin emeralds that were swimming in a sea of tears. "I'm looking."

"My eyes are the only mirrors that you need. I see you with my heart, David."

For a long moment he kept perfectly still, allowing her softly spoken words to wash over him, seeping into his consciousness. Then he released a breath he hadn't realized he was holding. And lifted a hand to cup the back of her neck, drawing her nearer to him until she was no longer kneeling, but lying next to him. Until there was no space separating his mouth, or his body, from hers.

His mouth clung to hers in passionate union. Minutes later, with an effort, she broke the kiss, her eyes once more fused to his. "The only thing I hate about your scars is the way you got them—with pain and suffering and trauma. I hate the fact that you could have died out there, alone. The scars on your face, your legs—they're like little borders, telling me that you were that far away from death. But they're all badges of courage, part of the man I love."

With that her mouth descended, her lips and tongue exquisitely sensual as she traced the path of each scar on his body. His eyes remained closed, his chest heaving, his heart beating in double time as he endured the erotic torture of her tender caress. "Open your eyes, David." And when he made no move to do so, Karen pressed her lips gently to his eyelids. "Open your eyes, my only love."

As his eyes fluttered open, she read messages of tenderness and longing in their deep blue depths. She lifted a hand to stroke the lean planes of his face. "Please, love me, David."

She could feel his hard arousal against the satin of her gown, felt her hips arch in response, as if her body was instinctively seeking its mate. She waited for his mouth, his hands, to touch her. He made no move at all. "What's wrong, love?" she asked in concern, wondering if the things she had said and done had somehow caused him pain.

"I'm afraid I'll hurt you," he said, his hand gently stroking her hair.

"You won't hurt me," she assured him.

Very slowly, almost reverently, David grasped Karen's shoulders, easing her down onto her back. At first he did nothing but look at her, his gaze sweeping the tempting hills and valleys of her slender body.

She blushed but did nothing to hamper his scrutiny.

He smiled in return, then bent his head, his mouth gently capturing her own, his tongue subtly invading the cavern of her mouth. Using only the lightest of touches, his hands traced the gowned slimness of her body, stroked the rounded curves, every movement a tender plea for acceptance. When his hand sought her breast, he was rewarded by the quickening of her breath. In slow motion his lips and tongue traced the V of the gown, then descended to worship her thrusting nipples through the thin fabric. At the same time his other hand traveled slowly downward, sliding past her narrow waist to caress the flatness of her belly, coming to rest at the source of her womanhood.

Her own hands weren't idle, intent on rediscovering the masculine body that hovered above her. Her hands slid beneath the cotton undershirt, seeking the hard planes of his chest. She felt his heart beat strongly against her seeking palms, felt him draw a shuddering breath as her hands reversed direction, pausing just above his waist, then coming around his back, where they rested on his tight buttocks.

Fighting for control, David slid the straps of the gown from her shoulders, bending his head so that his lips could follow the trail that his hands had blazed. He wooed her with hands, lips and tongue, working gently but urgently to arouse every part of her body.

She felt coolness on her skin, and realized she was no longer wearing the gown. As he stripped off his shirt and briefs, she gloried in his nakedness. Then, wanting to return some of the pleasure he'd given her, she urged him onto his back.

Karen lay practically on top of him as her mouth and tongue explored his chest, tasting the salt of his skin. She foraged through a forest of curling hair until her lips found his nipples, then teased them into hardened awareness. Using her uninjured left hand, she traced the muscular contours of his body, feeling his tense stillness as she worked her way past his ribs to the flat planes of his belly, and then to the heated maleness that pulsated with need.

"God, Karen!" he gasped, arching against her so that his velvet hardness insinuated itself between the moist junction of her thighs. "I want—to love you," he managed between tortured breaths.

Her mouth meshed with his, answering him without words.

Without removing his mouth from hers, he turned her so that once again she lay on her back. Then, very careful not to hurt her bruised body, he placed himself over her, propping himself on his elbows. Her legs parted, welcoming him.

And still he held back, entering her with exquisite tenderness as if she were made of the finest crystal, wanting only to give, not to take.

She wrapped her legs around his lean hips, arching herself against him in a silent plea for completion.

"Slow, love. Soft and slow," he breathed.

Sheathed tightly around him, held in his sensual embrace, she traveled heights and depths, until everything shattered, then came together. She was suspended in time and space, in a place of passion and pleasure and release she had never known before....

Afterward David lay on his back, keeping her with him, not wanting to release her from his arms. How long they drifted in a half world between sleeping and waking, he had no idea. Just before waking he dreamed of being stranded in the desert and then receiving droplets of life-giving moisture. Karen's arms encircled his waist, her face nestled in the hollow of his shoulder. And his skin was wet with her tears. He delicately licked at the salty moisture that clung to her lashes. "Why the tears, love?"

"Because it was so beautiful," she sighed against his warmth. "Because you make me feel so alive."

She opened tear-washed eyes as he reached for her left hand, his thumb caressing the backs of her ringless fingers.

"Will you do something for me?" he asked.

She said "Yes" without even waiting to find out what he wanted. "Anything."

"Carte blanche. That could be dangerous," he said with a half smile.

"I mean it."

As early as last September, as late as this January, he would never have considered asking Karen his next question. He would never have had the courage. Now, through love given and received, he could frame the words, difficult though they were. "Will you wear my ring—share my life? Marry me?"

For an answer, she put her arms around him, holding him to her breast. "I will," she breathed into his ear.

David shuddered in response as he whispered into the hollow of her breasts, "I like those two words. Keep practicing them for the marriage ceremony." Then, almost as an afterthought, he added, "At least I know you won't be marrying me for my looks."

"I don't believe you said that!" she marveled, amazed at the difference between the solitary man she had met in a shadowed rose garden and the tender lover who was now planning their future together, and gazing at her with a whimsical smile on his face, his heart in his eyes. She cradled his face lovingly between her hands. "Because you're wrong, David. So very wrong."

Though his blue eyes widened in puzzlement at her words, he was reassured by her healing touch.

"You are my love," she uttered in a fierce echo of the words she had once spoken in a wishful dream on a windswept mountaintop. Each syllable was punctuated with a kiss that seemed to penetrate to his very soul.

Her next words filled him with a sense of awe and wonder and humility. Because just before giving him a kiss that was overflowing with love and passion, she said, her voice hardly more than a whisper, "I *am* marrying you for your looks. And I love you just the way you are."

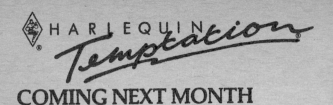

COMING NEXT MONTH

#277 THE ALL-AMERICAN MALE
Glenda Sanders

Tired of living in a fishbowl, heiress Cassaundra Snow was
determined to experience the "real" world. But posing as the
all-American working girl led her straight to Chuck
Granger, the all-American male—and a *very* real problem.
How could she ever explain to her prince that she was
actually Cinderella in reverse?

#278 'TIS THE SEASON
Vicki Lewis Thompson

Anna Tilford was longing for one of those storybook
Connecticut Christmases...ah, the peace. Until she met
her neighbor, who was supplying the official White House
Christmas tree. Of course, Sam Garrison had more than
just a green thumb going for him...and those other assets
definitely disturbed Anna's peace.

#279 LEGENDARY LOVER Renee Roszel

For thirteen years Tessa Jane Mankiller had nursed both a
grudge and a grand passion for Cord Redigo. Now that he'd
suddenly reappeared, she wasn't sure which response would
win out. But either way, Tessa knew she'd never be the same
when he left....

#280 MONTANA MAN Barbara Delinsky

Lily had known that starting a new life would be
tough. However, being stranded in a blizzard with her
month-old baby and a gruff cowboy named Quist was more
than she'd bargained for. But just as she was about to
succumb to panic, Lily realized that Quist was evoking
some completely unexpected and wonderfully
distracting emotions....

Especially for you,
Christmas from
HARLEQUIN HISTORICALS

An enchanting collection of three Christmas
stories by some of your favorite authors captures
the spirit of the season in the 1800s

TUMBLEWEED CHRISTMAS by Kristin James

A "Bah, humbug" Texas rancher meets his match in his
new housekeeper, a woman determined to bring the spirit
of a Tumbleweed Christmas into his life—and love into
his heart.

A CINDERELLA CHRISTMAS by Lucy Elliot

The perfect granddaughter, sister and aunt, Mary Hillyer
seemed destined for spinsterhood until Jack Gates arrived
to discover a woman with dreams and passions that were
meant to be shared during a Cinderella Christmas.

HOME FOR CHRISTMAS
by Heather Graham Pozzessere

The magic of the season brings peace Home For
Christmas when a Yankee captain and a Southern heiress
fall in love during the Civil War.

Look for HARLEQUIN HISTORICALS CHRISTMAS
STORIES in November wherever Harlequin books are sold.

Have You Ever Wondered If You Could Write A Harlequin Novel?

Here's great news—Harlequin is offering a series of cassette tapes to help you do just that. Written by Harlequin editors, these tapes give practical advice on how to make your characters—and your story—come alive. There's a tape for each contemporary romance series Harlequin publishes.

Mail order only

All sales final

HARLEQUIN'S "BIG WIN"
SWEEPSTAKES RULES & REGULATIONS
NO PURCHASE NECESSARY TO ENTER OR RECEIVE A PRIZE

1. To enter and join the Harlequin Reader Service, scratch off the pink metallic strips on all your BIG WIN tickets #1-#6. This will reveal the values for each sweepstakes entry number, the number of free books you will receive and your free bonus gift as part of our Reader Service. If you do not wish to take advantage of our introduction to the Harlequin Reader Service but wish to enter the Sweepstakes only, scratch off the pink metallic strips on your BIG WIN tickets #1-#4 only. To enter, return your entire sheet of tickets intact. Incomplete and/or inaccurate entries are not eligible for that section or section(s) of prizes. Not responsible for mutilated or unreadable entries or inadvertent printing errors. Mechanically reproduced entries are null and void. Be sure to also qualify for the Bonus Sweepstakes. See Rule #3 on how to enter.

2. Either way your unique Sweepstakes numbers will be compared against the list of winning numbers generated at random by the computer. In the event that all prizes are not claimed, random drawings will be held from all entries received from all presentations to award all unclaimed prizes. All cash prizes are payable in U.S. funds. This is in addition to any free, surprise or mystery gifts that might be offered. The following prizes are awarded in this sweepstakes: *Grand Prize (1) $1,000,000; First Prize (1) $35,000; Second Prize (1) $10,000; Third Prize (3) $5,000; Fourth Prize (10) $1,000; Fifth Prize (25) $500; Sixth Prize (5000)$5.

   *This Sweepstakes contains a Grand Prize offering of a $1,000,000 annuity. Winner may elect to receive $25,000 a year for 40 years without interest totalling $1,000,000 or $350,000 in one cash payment. Entrants may cancel Reader Service at any time without cost or obligation to buy (see details in center insert card).

3. Extra Bonus Prize: This presentation offers two extra bonus prizes valued at $30,000 each to be awarded in a random drawing from all entries received.

4. Versions of this Sweepstakes with different graphics will be offered in other mailings or at retail outlets by Torstar Corp. and its affiliates. This promotion is being conducted under the supervision of Marden-Kane, Inc., an independent judging organization. By entering this Sweepstakes, each entrant accepts and agrees to be bound by these rules and the decisions of the judges, which shall be final and binding. Odds of winning in the random drawing are dependent upon the total number of entries received. Taxes, if any, are the sole responsibility of the winners. Prizes are non-transferable. All entries must be received by March 31, 1990. The drawing will take place on or about April 30, 1990 at the offices of Marden-Kane, Inc., Lake Success, NY.

5. This offer is open to residents of the U.S., the United Kingdom and Canada, 18 years or older except employees of Torstar Corp., its affiliates, subsidiaries, Marden-Kane, Inc. and all other agencies and persons connected with conducting this Sweepstakes. All Federal, State and local laws apply. Void wherever prohibited or restricted by law.

6. Winners will be notified by mail and may be required to execute an affidavit of eligibility and release that must be returned within 14 days after notification. Canadian winners will be required to answer a skill-testing question. Winners consent to the use of their name, photograph and/or likeness for advertising and publicity in conjunction with this and similar promotions without additional compensation.

7. For a list of our most current major prize winners, send a stamped, self-addressed envelope to: WINNERS LIST c/o MARDEN-KANE, INC., P.O. BOX 701, SAYREVILLE, NJ 08871.

If Sweepstakes entry form is missing, please print your name and address on a 3" × 5" piece of plain paper and send to:

In the U.S.

Harlequin's "BIG WIN" Sweepstakes
901 Fuhrmann Blvd.
Box 1867
Buffalo, NY 14269-1867

In Canada

Harlequin's "BIG WIN" Sweepstakes
P.O. Box 609
Fort Erie, Ontario
L2A 5X3

© 1989 Harlequin Enterprises Limited   Printed in the U.S.A.

LTY-H119

Wonderful, luxurious gifts can be yours with proofs-of-purchase from any specially marked "Indulge A Little" Harlequin or Silhouette book with the Offer Certificate properly completed, plus a check or money order (do not send cash) to cover postage and handling payable to Harlequin/Silhouette "Indulge A Little, Give A Lot" Offer. We will send you the specified gift.

Mail-in-Offer

OFFER CERTIFICATE

Item:	A. Collector's Doll	B. Soaps in a Basket	C. Potpourri Sachet	D. Scented Hangers
# of Proofs-of -Purchase	18	12	6	4
Postage & Handling	$3.25	$2.75	$2.25	$2.00
Check One				

Name _____

Address _____ Apt. # _____

City _____ State _____ Zip _____

ONE PROOF OF PURCHASE

To collect your free gift by mail you must include the necessary number of proofs-of-purchase plus postage and handling with offer certificate.

HT-2

Harlequin®/Silhouette®

Mail this certificate, designated number of proofs-of-purchase and check or money order for postage and handling to:

INDULGE A LITTLE
P.O. Box 9055
Buffalo, N.Y. 14269-9055